GLIMMER TRAIN
STORIES

EDITORS
Susan Burmeister-Brown   Linda B. Swanson-Davies

CONSULTING EDITORS
Kimberly Bennett   Roz Wais
Chanda Wakefield

COPY EDITOR
Scott Stuart Allie

PROOFREADER
Rachel Penn

TYPESETTING & LAYOUT
Paul Morris

ADMINISTRATIVE ASSISTANT
Kaylin Elaine Dodge

COVER ARTIST
Jane Zwinger

STORY ILLUSTRATOR
Jon Leon

PUBLISHED QUARTERLY
in spring, summer, fall, and winter by **Glimmer Train Press, Inc.**
710 SW Madison Street, Suite 504, Portland, Oregon 97205-2900
Telephone: 503/221-0836   Facsimile: 503/221-0837
www.glimmertrain.com
PRINTED IN U.S.A.
Indexed in *The American Humanities Index.*

Glimmer Train (ISSN #1055-7520), registered in U.S. Patent and Trademark Office, is published quarterly, $32 per year in the U.S., by Glimmer Train Press, Inc., Suite 504, 710 SW Madison, Portland, OR 97205. Periodicals postage paid at Portland, OR, and additional mailing offices. POSTMASTER: Send address changes to Glimmer Train Press, Inc., Suite 504, 710 SW Madison, Portland, OR 97205.

ISSN # 1055-7520, **ISBN # 1-880966-41-7**, CPDA BIPAD # 79021

DISTRIBUTION: Bookstores can purchase *Glimmer Train Stories* through these distributors:
Ingram Periodicals, 1226 Heil Quaker Blvd., LaVergne, TN 37086
IPD, 674 Via de la Valle, #204, Solana Beach, CA 92075
Peribo PTY Ltd., 58 Beaumont Rd., Mt. Kuring-Gai, NSW 2080, AUSTRALIA
Ubiquity, 607 Degraw St., Brooklyn, NY 11217
SUBSCRIPTION SVCS: EBSCO, Faxon, Readmore, Turner Subscriptions, Blackwell's UK

Subscription rates: Order online (www.glimmertrain.com)
or by mail—one year, $32 within the U.S. (Visa/MC/check).
Airmail to Canada, $43; outside North America, $54.
Payable by Visa/MC or check for U.S. dollars drawn on a U.S. bank.

*Attention established and emerging short-story writers: We pay $500 for first publication and onetime anthology rights. **Visit our website for guidelines on submitting your work online.***

Glimmer Train Press also offers **Writers Ask**—*nuts, bolts, and informed perspectives— a quarterly newsletter for the committed writer. One year, four issues, $20 within the U.S. ($26 beyond the U.S.), Visa, MC, or check to Glimmer Train Press, Inc., or order online at www.glimmertrain.com.*

Dedication

It has been just over ten years now since our good friend Alan Silver died of metastatic melanoma at the age of thirty-six—far too young, none of us were ready to let him go. All of us in our thirties, still feeling the full spread of life stretching out ahead, and an overlooked mole on his back cut his time terribly short. It seemed absolutely impossible.

He was excited about our starting *Glimmer Train Stories*, and died one month after the first issue was published. His having been able to hold a real copy in his hands means a lot. Too many endeavors unfinished, but at least one would go on—and go on it does, here with our forty-second issue.

We dedicated our second issue to Alan, and asked our readers to keep an eye on their moles. Forty issues later, we do the same. If a mole changes, have it checked—don't wait.

We are missing you, Alan.

Linda & Susan

ONTENTS

CONTENTS

Monica Wood

Second grade. Eventually I grew into my head.

Monica Wood's most recent novel is *My Only Story*. *Ernie's Ark*, due out this spring, is a book of linked stories whose title story won a Pushcart Prize after appearing in *Glimmer Train*. "That One Autumn" is part of the collection. Two other books will appear this spring: *The Pocket Muse: Ideas and Inspirations for Writers*, and a paperback edition of her first novel, *Secret Language*.

Monica Wood

MONICA WOOD
That One Autumn

*T*hat one autumn, when Marie got to the cabin, something looked wrong. She took in the familiar view: the clapboard bungalow she and Ernie had inherited from his father, the bushes and trees that had grown up over the years, the dock pulled in for the season. She sat in the idling car, reminded of those "find the mistake" puzzles John used to pore over as a child, intent on locating mittens on the water skier, milk bottles in the parlor. Bent in a corner somewhere over the softening page, her blue-eyed boy would search for hours, convinced that after every wrong thing had been identified, more wrong things remained.

Sunlight pooled in the dooryard. The day gleamed, the clean Maine air casting a sober whiteness over everything. The gravel turn-around seemed vaguely disarranged. Scanning the line of spruce that shielded the steep slope to the lake's edge, Marie looked for movement. Behind the thick mesh screen of the front porch she could make out the wicker tops of the chairs. She turned off the ignition, trying to remember whether she'd taken time to straighten up the porch when she was last here, in early August, the weekend of Ernie's birthday. He and John had had one of their fights, and it was possible that in the ensuing clamor and silence she had forgotten to straighten up the porch. It was possible.

She got out of the car and checked around. Everything looked different after just a few weeks: the lake blacker through the part in the trees, the brown-eyed Susans gone weedy, the chairs on the porch definitely, definitely moved. Ernie had pushed a chair in frustration, she remembered. And John had responded in kind, upending the green one on his way out the door and down to the lake. They'd begun that weekend, like so many others, with such good intentions, only to discover anew how mismatched they were, parents to son. So, she had straightened the chairs—she had definitely straightened them—while outside Ernie's angry footsteps crackled over the gravel and, farther away, John's body hit the water in a furious smack.

She minced up the steps and pushed open the screen door, which was unlocked. "Hello?" she called out fearfully. The inside door was slightly ajar. *Take the dog,* Ernie had told her, *she'll be good company.* She wished now she had, though the dog, a Yorkie named Honey Girl, was a meek little thing and no good in a crisis. *I don't want company, Ernie. It's a week, it's forty miles, I'm not leaving you.* Marie was sentimental, richly so, which is why her wish to be alone after seeing John off to college had astonished them both. *But you're still weak,* Ernie argued. *Look how pale you are.* She packed a box of watercolors and a how-to book in her trunk as Ernie stood by, bewildered. *I haven't been alone in years,* she told him. *I want to find out what it feels like.* John had missed Vietnam by six merciful months, then he'd chosen Berkeley, as far from his parents as he could get, and now Marie wanted to be alone. Ernie gripped her around the waist and she took a big breath of him: man, dog, house, yard, mill. She had known him most of her life, and from time to time, when she could bear to think about it, she wondered whether their uncommon closeness was what had made their son a stranger.

You be careful, he called after her as she drove off. The words came back to her now as she peered through the partly open door at a wedge of kitchen she barely recognized. She saw jam jars open on the counter, balled-up dishtowels, a box of oatmeal upended and spilling a bit of oatmeal dust, a snaggled hairbrush, a red lipstick ground to a nub. Through the adjacent window she caught part of a rumpled sleeping bag in front of the fireplace, plus an empty glass and a couple of books.

Marie felt a little breathless, but not afraid, recognizing the disorder as strictly female. She barreled in, searching the small rooms like an angry, old-fashioned mother with a hickory switch. She found the toilet filled with urine, the back hall cluttered with camping gear, and the two bedrooms largely untouched except for a grease-stained knapsack thrown across Marie and Ernie's bed. By the time she got back out to the porch to scan the premises again, Marie had the knapsack in hand and sent it skidding across the gravel. The effort doubled her over, for Ernie was right: her body had not recovered from the thing it had suffered. As she held her stomach, the throbbing served only to stoke her fury.

Then she heard it: the sound of a person struggling up the steep, rocky path from the lake. Swishing grass. A scatter of pebbles. The subtle pulse of forward motion.

It was a girl. She came out of the trees into the sunlight, naked except for a towel bundled under one arm. Seeing the car, she stopped, then looked toward the cabin, where Marie uncoiled herself slowly, saying, "Who the hell are you?"

The girl stood there, apparently immune to shame. A delicate ladder of ribs showed through her paper-white skin. Her damp hair was fair and thin, her pubic hair equally thin and light. "Shit," she said. "Busted." Then she cocked her head, her face filled with a defiance Marie had seen so often in her own son that it barely registered.

"Cover yourself, for God's sake," Marie said.

The girl did, in her own good time, arranging the towel over her shoulders and covering her small breasts. Her walk was infuriatingly casual as she moved through the dooryard, picked up the knapsack, and sauntered up the steps, past Marie, and into the cabin. Marie followed her in. She smelled like the lake.

"Get out before I call the police," Marie said.

"Your phone doesn't work," the girl said peevishly. "And I can't say much for your toilet, either."

Of course nothing worked. They'd turned everything off, buttoned the place up after their last visit, John and Ernie at each other's throats as they hauled the dock up the slope, Ernie too slow on his end, John too fast on his, both of them arguing about whether or not Richard Nixon was a crook and should have resigned in disgrace.

"I said get out. This is my house."

The girl pawed through the knapsack. She hauled out a pair of panties and slipped them on. Then a pair of frayed jeans, and a mildewy shirt that Marie could smell across the room. As she toweled her hair it became lighter, nearly white. She leveled Marie with a look as blank and stolid as a pillar.

"I said get out," Marie snapped, jangling her car keys.

"I heard you."

"Then do it."

The girl dropped the towel on the floor, reached into the knapsack once more, extracted a comb, combed her flimsy, apparitional hair, and returned the comb. Then she pulled out a switchblade. It opened with a crisp, perfunctory snap.

"Here's the deal," she said. "I get to be in charge, and you get to shut up."

Marie shot out of the cabin and sprinted into the dooryard, where a bolt of pain brought her up short and windless. The girl was too quick in any case, catching Marie by the wrist before she could reclaim her breath. "Don't try anything," the girl said, her voice low and cold. "I'm unpredictable." She glanced around. "You expecting anybody?"

"No," Marie said, shocked into telling the truth.

"Then it's just us girls," she said, smiling a weird, thin smile that impelled Marie to reach behind her, holding the car for support. The girl presented her water-wrinkled palm and Marie forked over the car keys.

"Did you bring food?"

"In the trunk."

The girl held up the knife. "Stay right there."

Marie watched, terrified, as the girl opened the trunk and tore into a box of groceries, shoving a tomato into her mouth as she reached for some bread. A bloody trail of tomato juice sluiced down her neck.

Studying the girl—her quick, panicky movements—Marie felt her fear begin to settle into a morbid curiosity. This skinny girl seemed an unlikely killer; her tiny wrists looked breakable, and her stunning whiteness gave her the look of a child ghost. In a matter of seconds, a thin, reluctant vine of maternal compassion twined through Marie and burst into violent bloom.

"When did you eat last?" Marie asked her.

"None of your business," the girl said, cramming her mouth full of bread.

"How old are you?"

The girl finished chewing, then answered: "Nineteen. What's it to you?"

"I have a son about your age."

"Thrilled to know it," the girl said, handing a grocery sack to Marie. She herself hefted the box and followed Marie into the cabin, her bare feet making little animal sounds on the gravel. Once inside, she ripped into a box of Cheerios.

"Do you want milk with that?" Marie asked her.

All at once the girl welled up, and she nodded, wiping her eyes with the heel of one hand, turning her head hard right, hard left, exposing her small, translucent ears. "This isn't me," she sniffled. She lifted the knife, but did not give it over. "It's not even mine."

"Whose is it?" Marie said steadily, pouring milk into a bowl.

"My boyfriend's." The girl said nothing more for a few minutes, until the cereal was gone, another bowl poured, and that, too, devoured. She wandered over to the couch, a convertible covered with anchors that Ernie had bought to please John, who naturally never said a word about it.

"Where is he, your boyfriend?" Marie asked finally.

"Out getting supplies." The girl looked up quickly, a snap of the eyes revealing something Marie thought she understood.

"How long's he been gone?"

The girl waited. "Day and a half."

Marie nodded. "Maybe his car broke down."

"That's what I wondered." The girl flung a spindly arm in the general direction of the kitchen. "I'm sorry about the mess. My boyfriend's hardly even paper-trained."

"Then maybe you should think about getting another boyfriend."

"I told him, no sleeping on the beds. We didn't sleep on your beds."

"Thank you," Marie said.

"It wasn't my idea to break in here."

"I'm sure it wasn't."

"He's kind of hiding out, and I'm kind of with him."

"I see," Marie said, scanning the room for weapons: fireplace poker, dictionary, curtain rod. She couldn't imagine using any of these things on the girl, whose body appeared held together with thread.

"He knocked over a gas station. Two, actually, in Portland."

"That sounds serious."

She smiled a little. "He's a serious guy."

"You could do better, don't you think?" Marie asked. "Pretty girl like you."

The girl's big eyes narrowed. "How old are *you*?"

"Thirty-eight."

"You look younger."

"Well, I'm not," Marie said. "My name is Marie, by the way."

"I'm Tracey."

"Tell me, Tracey," Marie said. "Am I your prisoner?"

"Only until he gets back. We'll clear out after that."

"Where are you going?"

"Canada. Which is where he should've gone about six years ago."

"A vet?"

Tracey nodded. "War sucks."

"Well, now, that's extremely profound."

"Don't push your luck, Marie," Tracey said. "It's been a really long week."

They spent the next hours sitting on the porch, Marie thinking furiously in a chair, Tracey on the steps, the knife glinting in her fist. At one point Tracey stepped down into the gravel, dropped her jeans, and squatted over the spent irises, keeping Marie in her sights the whole time. Marie, who had grown up in a different era entirely, found this fiercely embarrassing. A wind came up on the lake; a pair of late loons called across the water. The only comfort Marie could manage was that the boyfriend, whom she did not wish to meet, not at all, clearly had run out for good. Tracey seemed to know this, too, chewing on her lower lip, facing the dooryard as if the hot desire of her stare could make him materialize.

"What's his name?" Marie asked.

"None of your business. We met in a chemistry class." She smirked at Marie's surprise. "Pre-med."

"Are you going back to school?"

Tracey threw back her head and cackled, showing two straight rows of excellent teeth. "Yeah, right. He's out there right now paying our pre-registration."

Marie composed herself, took some silent breaths. "It's just that I find it hard to believe—"

"People like you always do," Tracey said. She slid Marie a look. "You're never willing to believe the worst of someone."

Marie closed her eyes, wanting Ernie. She imagined him leaving work about now, coming through the mill gates with his lunch bucket and cap, shoulders bowed at the prospect of

J. LEON 01—

the empty house. She longed to be waiting there, to sit on the porch with him over a pitcher of lemonade, comparing days, which hadn't changed much over the years, really, but always held some ordinary pleasures. Today they would have wondered about John, thought about calling him, decided against it.

"You married?" Tracey asked, as if reading her mind.

"Twenty years. We met in seventh grade."

"Then what are you doing up here alone?"

"I don't know," Marie said. But suddenly she did, she knew exactly, looking at this girl who had parents somewhere waiting.

"I know what you're thinking," the girl said.

"You couldn't possibly."

"You're wondering how a nice girl like me ended up like this." When Marie didn't answer, she added, "Why do you keep doing that?"

"What?"

"That." The girl pointed to Marie's hand, which was making absent semicircles over her stomach. "You pregnant?"

"No," Marie said, withdrawing her hand. But she had been, shockingly, for most of the summer; during John's final weeks at home, she had been pregnant. Back then her hand had gone automatically to the womb, that strange, unpredictable vessel, as she and Ernie nuzzled in bed, dazzled by their change in fortune. For nights on end they made their murmured plans, lost in a form of drunkenness, waiting for John to skulk through the back door long past curfew, when they would rise from their nestled sheets to face him—their first child now, not their only—his splendid blue eyes glassy with what she hoped were the normal complications of adolescence, equal parts need and contempt.

They did not tell him about the pregnancy, and by the first of September it was over prematurely, Marie balled into a heap on their bed for three days, barely able to open her swollen eyes. "Maybe it's for the best," Ernie whispered to her, petting her curled back. They could hear John ramming around in the kitchen downstairs, stocking the cupboards with miso and bean curd and other things they'd never heard of, counting off his last days in the house by changing everything in it. As Ernie kissed her sweaty head, Marie rested her hand on the freshly scoured womb that had held their second chance. "It might not have been worth it," Ernie whispered, words that staggered her so thoroughly that she bolted up, mouth agape, asking, "What did you say, Ernie? Did you just say something?" Their raising of John had, after all, been filled with fine wishes for the boy; it was not their habit to acknowledge disappointment, or regret, or sorrow. As the door downstairs clicked shut on them and John faded into another night with his mysterious friends, Marie turned to her husband, whom she loved, God help her, more than she loved her son. *Take it back*, she wanted to tell him, but he mistook her pleading look entirely. "She might've broken our hearts," he murmured. "I can think of a hundred ways." He was holding her at the time, speaking softly, almost to himself, and his hands on her felt like the meaty intrusion of some stranger who'd just broken into her bedroom. "Ernie, stop there," she told him, and he did.

It was only now, imprisoned on her own property by a skinny girl who belonged back in chemistry class, that Marie understood that she had come here alone to find a way to forgive him. What did he mean, not worth it? Worth what? Was he speaking of John?

Marie looked down over the trees into the lake. She and Ernie had been twenty years old when John was born. You think you're in love now, her sister warned, but wait till you meet your baby—implying that married love would look bleached and pale by contrast. But John was a sober, suspicious baby, vaguely intimidating; and their fascination for him became one more thing they had in common. As their child became more and more himself, a cryptogram they couldn't decipher, Ernie and Marie's bungled affections and wayward exertions revealed less of him and more of themselves.

Ernie and Marie, smitten since seventh grade: it was a story they thought their baby son would grow up to tell their grandchildren. At twenty they had thought this. She wanted John to remember his childhood the way she liked to: a soft-focus, greeting-card recollection in which Ernie and Marie strolled hand in hand in a park somewhere with the fruit of their desire frolicking a few feet ahead. But now she doubted her own memory. John must have frolicked on occasion. Certainly he must have frolicked. But at the present moment she could conjure only a lumbering resignation, as if he had already tired of their story before he broke free of the womb. They would have been more ready for him now, she realized. She was in a position now to love Ernie less, if that's what a child required.

The shadow of the spruces arched long across the dooryard. Dusk fell.

Tracey got up. "I'm hungry again. You want anything?"

"No, thanks."

Tracey waited. "You have to come in with me."

Marie stepped through the door first, then watched as Tracey made herself a sandwich. "I don't suppose it's crossed your mind that your boyfriend might not come back," Marie said.

Tracey took a big bite. "No, it hasn't."

"If I were on the run I'd run alone, wouldn't you? Don't you think that makes sense?"

Chewing daintily, Tracey flattened Marie with a luminous, eerily knowing look. "Are you on the run, Marie?"

"What I'm saying is that he'll get a lot farther a lot faster without another person to worry about."

Tracey swallowed hard. "Well, what I'm saying is you don't know shit about him. Or me, for that matter. So you can just shut up."

"I could give you a ride home."

"Not without your keys, you couldn't." She opened the fridge and gulped some milk from the bottle. "If I wanted to go home I would've gone home a long time ago."

It had gotten dark in the cabin. Marie flicked on the kitchen light. She and Ernie left the electricity on year-round because it was more trouble not to, and occasionally they came here in winter to snowshoe through the long, wooded alleys. It was on their son's behalf that they had come to such pastimes, on their son's behalf that the cabin had filled over the years with well-thumbed guidebooks to butterflies and insects and fish and birds. But John preferred his puzzles by the fire, his long, furtive vigils on the dock, leaving it to his parents to discover the world. They turned up pine cones, strips of birch bark for monogramming, once a speckled feather from a pheasant. John inspected these things indifferently, listened to parental homilies on the world's breathtaking design, all the while maintaining the demeanor of a good-hearted homeowner suffering the encyclopedia salesman's pitch.

"Why don't you want to go home?" Marie asked. "Really, I'd like to know." She was remembering the parting scene at the airport, John uncharacteristically warm, allowing her to hug him as long as she wanted, thanking her for an all-purpose "everything" that she could fill in as she pleased for years to come. Ernie, his massive arms folded in front of him, welled up, nodding madly. But as John disappeared behind the gate Ernie clutched her hand, and she knew what he knew: that their only son, their first and only child, was not coming back. He would finish school, find a job in California, call them twice a year.

"My father's a self-righteous blowhard, if you're dying to know," Tracey said. "And my mother's a doormat."

"Maybe they did the best they could."

"Maybe they didn't."

"Maybe they tried in ways you can't know about."

Tracey looked Marie over. "My mother's forty-two," she said. "She would've crawled under a chair the second she saw the knife."

Marie covered the mustard jar and returned it to the fridge. "It's possible, Tracey, that your parents never found the key to you."

Tracey seemed to like this interpretation of her terrible choices. Her shoulders softened some. "So where's this son of yours, anyway?"

"We just sent him off to Berkeley."

Tracey smirked a little. "Uh-oh."

"What's that supposed to mean?" Marie asked. "What do you mean?"

"Berkeley's a pretty swinging place. You don't send sweet little boys there."

"I never said he was a sweet little boy," Marie said, surprising herself. But it was true: her child had never been a sweet little boy.

"You'll be lucky if he comes back with his brain still working."

"I'll be lucky if he comes back at all."

Tracey frowned. "You're messing with my head, right? Poor, tortured mother? You probably don't even have kids." She folded her arms. "But if you do have a kid, and he's at Berkeley, prepare yourself."

"Look, Tracey," Marie said irritably, "why don't you just take my car? If you're so devoted to this boyfriend of yours, why not go after him?"

"Because I'd have no idea where to look, and you'd run to

the nearest police station." Tracey finished the sandwich and rinsed the plate, leading Marie to suspect that someone had at least taught her to clean up after herself. The worst parent in the world can at least do that. John had lovely manners, and she suddenly got a comforting vision of him placing his scraped plate in a cafeteria sink.

"The nearest police station is twenty miles from here," Marie said.

"Well, that's good news, Marie, because look who's back."

Creeping into the driveway, one headlight out, was a low-slung, mud-colored Valiant with a cracked windshield. The driver skulked behind the wheel, blurry as an inkblot. When Tracey raced out to greet him, the driver opened the door and emerged as a jittery shadow. The shadow flung itself toward the cabin as Marie fled for the back door and banged on the lock with her fists.

In moments he was upon her, a wiry man with a powerful odor and viselike hands. He half-carried her back to the kitchen as she fell limp with panic. Then, like a ham actor in a silent movie, he lashed her to a kitchen chair with cords of filthy rawhide.

"You wanna tell me how the fuck we get rid of her?" he snarled at Tracey, whose apparent fright gave full flower to Marie's budding terror. That he was handsome—dark eyed, square jawed, with full, shapely lips—made him all the more terrifying.

"What was I supposed to do?" Tracey quavered. "Listen, I kept her here for a whole day with no—"

"Where's your keys?" he roared at Marie.

"Here, they're here," Tracey said, fumbling them out of her pocket. "Let's go, Mike, please, let's just go."

"You got money?" he asked, leaning over Marie, one cool strand of his long hair raking across her bare arm. She could hardly breathe, looking into his alarming, moist eyes.

"My purse," she gasped. "In the car."

He stalked out, his dirty jeans sagging at the seat, into which someone had sewn a facsimile of the American flag. He looked near starving, his upper arms shaped like bedposts, thin and tapering and hard. She heard the car door open and the contents of her purse spilling over the gravel.

"The pre-med was a lie," Tracey said. "I met him at a concert." She darted a look outside, her lip quivering. "You know how much power I have over my own life, Marie?" She lifted her hand and squeezed her thumb and index finger together. "This much."

He was in again, tearing into the fridge, cramming food into his mouth. The food seemed to calm him some. He looked around. He could have been twenty-five or forty-five, a man weighted by bad luck and a mean spirit that encased his true age like barnacles on a boat. "Pick up our stuff," he said to Tracey. "We're out of this dump."

Tracey did as he said, gathering the sleeping bag and stuffing it into a sack. He watched her body damply as she moved; Marie felt an engulfing nausea but could not move herself, not even to cover her mouth at the approaching bile. Her legs were lashed to the chair legs, her arms tied behind her, giving her a deeply discomfiting sensation of being bound to empty space. She felt desperate to close her legs, cross her arms over her breasts, unwilling to die with her most womanly parts exposed. "I'm going to be sick," she gulped, but it was too late, a thin trail of spit and bile lolloping down her shirt front.

Mike lifted his forearm, dirty with tattoos, and chopped it down across Marie's jaw. She thumped backward to the floor, chair and all, tasting blood, seeing stars, letting out a squawk of despair. Then she fell silent, looking at the upended room, stunned. She heard the flick of a switchblade and felt the heat of his shadow. She tried to snap her eyes shut, to wait for what came next, but they opened again, fixed on his; in the still, shiny irises she searched for a sign of latent goodness, or regret, some long-ago time that defined him. In the sepulchral silence she locked eyes with him, sorrow to sorrow. He dropped the knife. "Fuck this, you do it," he said to Tracey, then swaggered out. She heard her car revving in the dooryard, the radio blaring on. Now her eyes closed. A small rustle materialized near her left ear; it was Tracey, crouching next to her, holding the opened blade.

"Shh," Tracey said. "He's a coward, and he doesn't like blood, but he's not above beating the hell out of me." She patted Marie's cheek. "So let's just pretend I've killed you."

Marie began to weep, silently, a sheen of moisture beading beneath her eyes. She made a prayer to the Virgin Mary, something she had not done since she was a child. She summoned an image of Ernie sitting on the porch, missing her. Of John scraping that plate in the college cafeteria. With shocking tenderness, Tracey made a small cut near Marie's temple just above the hairline. It hurt very little, but the blood began to course into her hair in warm, oozy tracks. Tracey lifted the knife, now a rich, dripping red. "You'll be okay," she said. "But head wounds bleed like crazy." The horn from Marie's car sounded in two long, insistent blasts.

"You chose a hell of a life for yourself, Tracey," Marie whispered.

"Yeah," Tracey said, closing her palm lightly over the knife. She got up. "But at least I chose."

"You don't know anything about me."

"Ditto. Take care."

For much of the long evening Marie kept still, blinking into the approaching dark. She had to pee desperately but determined to hold it even if it killed her, which she genuinely thought it might. She was facing the ceiling, still tied, the blood on her face and hair drying uncomfortably. She recalled John's childhood habit of hanging slothlike from banisters or chair backs, loving the upside-down world. Perhaps his parents were easier to understand this way. She saw now what had so compelled him: the ceiling would make a marvelous floor, a creamy expanse you could navigate however you wished; you could fling yourself from corner to corner, unencumbered except for an occasional light fixture. Even the walls looked inviting: the windows appeared to open from the top down, the tops of doors made odd, amusing steps into the next room, framed pictures floated knee high, their reversed images full of whimsy, hard to decode. In time she got used to the overturned room, even preferred it. It calmed her. She no longer felt sick. She understood that Ernie was on his way here, of course he was, he would be here before the moon rose, missing her, full of apology for disturbing her peace, but he needed her, the house was empty and their son was gone and he needed her as he steered down the dirt road, veering left past the big boulder, entering the dooryard to find a strange, battered car and a terrifying silence.

"Oh, Ernie," she said when he did indeed panic through the door. "Ernie. Sweetheart. Untie me." In he came, just as she knew he would.

And then? They no longer looked back on this season as the autumn when they lost their second child. This season—with its gentle temperatures and propensity for inspiring flight—they recalled instead as that one autumn when those awful people, that terrible pair, broke into the cabin. They exchanged one memory for the other, remembering Ernie's raging, man-sized sobs as he worked at the stiff rawhide, remembering him rocking her under a shaft of moonlight that sliced through the door he'd left open, remembering, half-laughing, that the first thing Marie wanted to do, after being rescued by her prince, was pee. This moment became the turning point—this moment and no other—when two long-married people decided to stay married, to succumb to the shape of the rest of their life, to live with things they would not speak of. They shouldered each other into the coming years because there was no other face each could bear to look at in this moment of turning, no other arms they could bear but each other's, and they made themselves right again, they did, just the two of them.

KENT HARUF
Writer

Interview

by Jim Nashold

Kent Haruf was born the son of a Methodist minister in 1943 in Pueblo, Colorado. He graduated from Nebraska Wesleyan University in 1965 and for the next two years worked in the Peace Corps, where he began writing short stories. After returning to the United States, he continued to teach himself the craft of fiction while holding down odd jobs as a farm laborer, hospital orderly, railroad worker, librarian, and orphanage house parent.

His first novel, The Tie that Binds, *was published in 1984, and garnered a Whiting Award and a special citation from the PEN/Hemingway Foundation for first fiction. His work has appeared in* Puerto Del Sol, Gettysburg Review, Grand Street, *and* Prairie Schooner, *and was recognized in* Best

Photo credit: Jim Nashold

Kent Haruf

American Short Stories *(1987) and* Where Past Meets
Present: Modern Colorado Short Stories *(1993). His
second novel,* Where You Once Belonged, *was published in
1990 to critical praise.*

*Haruf taught creative writing at Southern Illinois University
in Carbondale for nine years and now lives in Colorado. In
1999, after six years of work, Knopf published his third novel,*
Plainsong, *which received widespread acclaim. The novel was a
finalist for a number of awards including the National Book
Award, the* New Yorker's *Best Fiction Award, and the* Los
Angeles Times *Best Fiction Award. It was the winner of the
American Library Association's Alex Award for Best Fiction, the
Mountains and Plains Booksellers Award, the Midlands Authors
Award, and the Salon.com Fiction Award. Two of Haruf's
novels,* Plainsong *and* The Tie that Binds, *have been optioned
for television movies by CBS. He is currently at work on a fourth
novel.*

Where did you grow up?
    I grew up in the northeast corner of Colorado in the high-
plains and short-grass prairie. I lived out there until I was
eleven or twelve. My father was a Methodist preacher and we
moved around in towns all with a population of two thousand
or less. The towns were named Holyoke, Wray, and Yuma. I
lived there again when I was an adult, and I taught school out
in that part of the state for eight years in the most rural school
district in Colorado. It's a part of the country and part of the
world which I call home, and which I have an emotional and
almost holy response to when I reenter it. It's not pretty, but in
my view it's beautiful and you have to know how to look at it.
Most people drive across it as fast as they can to get to Denver
or the mountains, but if you grew up there it feels like home.
There's plenty to see. It sort of teaches you how to slow down.
Teaches you how to pay attention.

26   *Glimmer Train Stories*

What was living there like?

It was an idyllic place to grow up. It was somewhat like Mark Twain writes about Hannibal, Missouri, back in the 1840s. We had friends who had horses and we rode nearly every day in the summer. My parents let us grow up on our own. They didn't restrict us in any unnecessary way.

What were some of the books you remember reading?

As a kid I read books that weren't great literature, but I read all the time. I read a lot of Western stories about horses and cowboys, all the Black Stallion series, *Green Grass of Wyoming*, *Thunderhead*, and *My Friend Flicka*. I was very much interested in Western stories at that time.

Were your parents readers or storytellers?

My parents read a good deal every day. My dad read mostly biographies and history and newspapers. My mom read fiction, and also read us parts of novels when we traveled to my grandparents' place in South Dakota. My father was a great storyteller, and told stories after dinner. The stories I enjoyed the most were about his own background growing up on a homestead in North Dakota, and about ranch life. As a family, when we were on vacation, we took turns telling stories. Somebody would start, then somebody else would pick it up and move it on. So that was part of our entertainment.

When did you decide you wanted to be a writer?

When I was in college I began to read Faulkner and Hemingway, two writers that changed my life. I hadn't read anything so shockingly wonderful as those two writers, and what they could do on the page stunned me. I've never gotten over that shock, and don't want to. So I began to know about my middle college years that I wanted to do something with literature, and I began to write. But I didn't become intense about writing until after college when I was in the Peace Corps. I was in a pretty isolated situation and I began to write on my own in Turkey.

Were there specific stories of Faulkner's and Hemingway's that made a big impact?

Hemingway's Nick Adams stories were important. "The Snows of Kilimanjaro," "The Killers," and "In Another Country" made a huge impact. Then we read *The Sun Also Rises* and *A Farewell to Arms.* With Faulkner, "The Bear" made a huge and immediate impact on me, and *The Sound and the Fury.* It's hard to explain, but it was almost overwhelming, like a religious experience, to have read those kind of things at that age.

Was it the stories or the language that impressed you the most?

Both. In Hemingway's case, the language and that cleanliness of prose, and that absolutely clean, precise way of telling something was evocative and interesting. In Faulkner's case it was his style and his writing about rural America which I had never read before. I was bowled over by the stories and by his enormous skill.

What caused you to go into the Peace Corps?

I wanted to get out of the United States. Since I had no money, the Peace Corps was a way to see different parts of the world. I wanted to especially go to the Middle East.

You were teaching English as a second language in Turkey. Where specifically did you live?

I was out on the Anatolian plateau in the very small village of Felahiye. It was a place of about two thousand people, very much like the places I grew up in. I taught English to kids in the middle school. It was of great value to me since it was a time of reflection and self-examination. I was alone and read a lot, and began to keep a regular journal and to try and write fiction and figure out some things about myself.

So you made your first attempts at fiction in Turkey. Was that out of a sense of loneliness or out of wanting to be a writer, or both?

Both, probably, but more out of a desire to write something of value. But the things I wrote were just abysmal, just awful.

After Turkey, you traveled around that summer. Was it 1967 or '68?

It was the summer of '67.

Did you get to the Middle East?

I traveled around in Turkey and then went through Bulgaria, Yugoslavia, and up into Italy, Austria, and Germany.

Did you get to Paris?

I didn't. I stayed away from France. I spent quite a lot of time in Austria and Holland, especially Amsterdam. I stayed away from Paris because I knew no French and I understood it was difficult to get around without some knowledge of the language. And maybe I didn't want to be disillusioned by what I'd read about Hemingway in Paris in the twenties.

After going to Turkey, did you set your sights on going to Iowa, or did it happen later?

While I was in Turkey I did apply to the Iowa Writers' Workshop, and wasn't accepted. I applied again when I was about twenty-eight or twenty-nine. I was so desperate to get there that I moved to Iowa City and took a job as a janitor in an old-folks' home and waited. Later, I moved my wife and daughter out there. Then, in May, they said they'd take me, and I was one of the very last applicants they accepted that year.

Who was head of the Iowa Writers' Workshop at the time?

The director was a man named Jack Leggett. I never took any classes with him, but he was a good guy and a serious writer. I took classes that first year with Seymour Krim, a nonfiction writer. Second semester I studied with Dan Wakefield, a fiction writer, and I took some fiction-writing classes with Ben Santos, who was important to me. But it wasn't so much what those men were saying in class or doing, but more taking writing seriously, and being in a place where you were expected to write; being with other people who were writing, and trying to pay attention to what you needed to do. I got out of that program what I needed to without

some formal training. It was a matter of intense concentration, getting some encouragement, and getting some reaction
to what I was writing—having some notion of where I was
doing something right on the page and where I wasn't. In the
second year I took classes with Vance Bourjaily, who was very
good, and then the last semester I studied with John Irving.

*Was the teaching style of Dan Wakefield different from John
Irving's?*

In my memory they taught in many of the same ways. Like
myself, they didn't get into messing around in the manuscript
very much. In fact, I never had a single conference with either
one of them. It was more a *laissez-faire* way of teaching. They
said here's where you're doing something right and here's
where you're doing something wrong. It was up to you to
figure out what to do about it. They never made any
significant suggestions about your work, but when they said
you were doing something right and they were honest about
it, it was tremendously encouraging. I felt I was working hard
on my own with my writing and they were sort of distant
midwives.

Did other students have much influence on your writing?

You got a whole variety of responses to what you'd done,
and you began pretty quickly to know which students to trust
in regard to what they said. There were some very good
student writers there, some people who have made wonderful
careers since then. Tracy Kidder, Stuart Dybek, Denis Johnson,
Thom Jones, Tom Boyle, and Jane Smiley.

Is writing something that can be taught?

Some aspects of writing can be taught. On the assumption
there's some talent, you help students discover what their
material is and how to approach that material, and to deal
with matters of craft in terms of developing characters, how
to say things that are vivid and evocative, and how to tell
when they're not doing those things.

For your thesis at Iowa, you had written part of a novel. This was accepted by a publisher in New York, but they eventually decided not to publish it.

I signed an option with Harper Row for the book I was working on during my last year. When I finished it, they didn't take it. Rhoda Weyr, a literary agent, worked very hard to place that book, but wasn't able to. I was very disappointed, discouraged, and bitter about that.

What was the story about?

The story was autobiographical and had to do with my family. I'm glad it wasn't published. It didn't deserve to be, because it wasn't nearly good enough. But what I did discover in that book was a chapter set in Holt, Colorado, which was when I first came to use that name for a town. I discovered what I wanted to write about in one of those chapters of that novel.

So it wasn't a wasted effort.

No.

You've mentioned that you used Faulkner's idea of taking your own patch of earth you grew up on, and concentrating on that, and never being able to exhaust it.

Very much so.

How did you come up with the idea for your first published novel, The Tie that Binds*?*

My older brother, Verne, had a ranch out in northeast Colorado, and one time I was out there riding around with him in his pickup, and we'd been out checking some cattle. He mentioned that a quarter of a mile away was a house where an old brother and sister lived. A couple years later I began to write about it. What came to my imagination was an old brother and sister living alone out in the country of Colorado in an old yellow house surrounded by weeds. What I knew from the outset was how they would die, and that's all I knew. Rethinking that story, I wondered why they'd end up that way. So I invented their past, and then a male voice who became the narrator, Sanders Roscoe, and he had to have a history and a family. Out of those narrative necessities came the texture of that novel.

So when you describe the beginning of that book, it's the combination of character and place that's the seed of a story.

Exactly.

Was that true of the second and third novels also?

I always come first to character, because I already know I want to write about northeast Colorado. These characters become full blown, so that when I actually begin writing, they are fully integrated people. My effort is to get them down on the page as complexly and as fully as I know them.

Themes in your first novel reappear in all your books. Old people living alone, the harshness of ranch life, thwarted love, losing one family and gaining another, and the idea of violence and love being intertwined. These are specific themes that surface again in Plainsong.

I don't set out to consciously write a story about any one thing. What I'm trying to do is to write a story about characters who interest me and whose stories I want to tell. I don't feel very competent talking about what comes out of these stories. What you say seems plausible, but I promise you I had no notion in the composition of those books to write about specific themes.

When you wrote that first book, it seemed like it grew as you worked on it. Do you write all the way through in one draft and then revise, or do you polish as you go along?

I do the latter. I'm not sure it's a method I recommend, but I'm sure I'm not the only writer who works that way. My habit is to perfect individual sentences, individual paragraphs, and individual pages, and when I think they're as good as I can make them, I feel free to go on to the next part. So when I write the last sentence of the last paragraph, I'm done with the book.

Your first book is a quiet but powerful story because the characters are so strong and their relationships are so claustrophobic. Is this the feeling one gets about life in the high plains where people live in physical isolation?

There is a kind of isolation. But maybe that's my character. I may have felt that same way if I'd grown up in Chicago. It's a paradox. Out in the plains you can see forever. You can see your neighbors, their houses, and there's nothing hiding them. You can see people working out in the barnyard. Yet there's this distance between you that's unbridgable, and that's very interesting to me.

One of the main characters in The Tie that Binds *is Roy Goodnough, the patriarch of the family. He's a tough, unforgiving character, determined to survive on his own terms. Is he drawn from people that you encountered, like other cowboys or ranchers?*

Not so much, really. I don't think I've had much experience with people like Roy, except that I've had some intimation of them. I don't want him to seem monstrous. He has to seem human in his fierceness. The awful thing for him is that he has this tremendous drive to succeed as a farmer/rancher on his own terms, and yet because he has lost his fingers he depends on other people. That is a kind of handicap and malady that he doesn't know how to deal with in a very human way.

Even though he comes through as a bastard, you feel sympathy and pity for him.

The scene where Sanders sees his father after a fistfight with the old man, carrying him into the bedroom to clean him up and take the sand burrs out of his clothes, you see the old man almost tearful. That's the moment that Sanders feels genuine sympathy for him, and perhaps through Sanders the reader will feel something human about him.

The title The Tie that Binds *describes the relationship between Edith and Roy Goodnough. Why does she stick around when her father's a bastard?*

I want to think that Edith, even though she's sacrificed a great deal, is not implausible either. She acts out of virtue, loyalty, courage, and self-sacrifice. Those values are not talked about these days, but they still seem to be elemental virtues worth writing about.

The women in all your books seem psychologically stronger than the men.

They provide the traditional function of nurturers and people who hold society together and connect everybody in their relationships. But they also are enormously strong and courageous. I'd include Maggie Jones, the teacher in *Plainsong*, among those characters. She's at the very heart of that novel, and connects everybody else. She's the catalyst, the wise, loving, strong part of that storm.

There's quite a bit of understated humor in your books. In The Tie that Binds, *one of the funniest scenes is when Edith is milking the cows and the cow's tail slaps her in the face.*

I intended that to be funny, and corrective of the romantic notion that milking cows is glorious or fun. Part of it was also my own revenge for when I milked cows as a way of making a living for my family once. It was a good education, and it was hard work. I started milking at three in the morning and went back again at three or four in the afternoon. What I describe in that scene actually happened to me. An old cow wrapped her tail around my head and I wanted to kill her. So it was my literary revenge on an actual cow.

You lovingly recreate the detail of ranch life, which is fast disappearing. Such details as cutting hay or taking care of cattle are integral parts of your writing.

I've been interested in ranch life since I was a kid and heard my dad talk about it and then spent time with my brother on his ranch. I do know something about that, but I'm no expert. It's very important to me to get those details accurate. The passage of the cow wrapping her tail around my head was read aloud to me by a dairyman on New Year's Eve. We were both drunk enough that he called me out to the kitchen, opened *The Tie that Binds*, and read that passage to me, and then stabbed his finger on the page and said, "That's exactly right, goddammit." That to me was the greatest compliment I've ever had, because it came from somebody who knew exactly what I was writing about and who was an expert.

What time of day do you like to write, and what are your habits?

My habit is to write in the morning. I start by eight-thirty and work till noon. When I'm working on a novel I will do that six and seven days a week. My practice is to begin by making a few notes in a journal about the weather and about what happened the day before. Then I read something by some classic writer. Most of that reading is of Faulkner, Hemingway, or Conrad. I read things which I've read before and don't have to think about what the story line is or what my feelings are about it. So what I'm trying to do is get my mind into some vein of fiction. Then I begin to look over what I've written the day before and make changes in that, and gradually work up to writing new material. So, it's a process of bringing me back in touch with what I've been writing, and inching the novel ahead each day.

Do you produce a paragraph or several paragraphs in that amount of time?

It varies, but if I write several paragraphs a day I feel pretty good about that. I don't think I've written more than a page or two at a single sitting.

And you're working through these drafts on a typewriter.

I start out making notes on paper with a pen or pencil, and then I use old, yellow paper called "seconds" to do a first draft on my typewriter. When I do this first draft, I shut the lights off and pull a stocking cap over my head and eyes, and I'm typing blind. It's the old paradox that you see by blinding yourself. I do that for a couple reasons. One is that the second book, *Where You Once Belonged,* I wrote on a computer, and I never felt good about it, so I wanted to get back to using a manual typewriter. It's also an effort to stop rewriting sentences endlessly. I'm also trying to get in touch with some subliminal or subconscious thinking and not be distracted by punctuation, grammar, spelling, or sentence structure.

You mentioned that Hemingway and Faulkner had big influences on your career. What other writers have been important to you?

I read a lot of Flannery O'Connor at one time, and I've read Ray Carver thoroughly. I read all of Steinbeck and went through a Russian phase reading Tolstoy and Dostoevsky, and more recently I've been reading a lot of Chekhov. Conrad, I like. Eudora Welty's been significant to me. The Canadian writer Alice Munro is one of the greatest living writers. At one time I thought *The Stranger* was a great novel. I studied Sherwood Anderson's *Winesburg, Ohio,* and liked it tremendously, and also liked Ford Maddox Ford's *The Good Soldier.*

How much of your fiction is autobiographical?

You can't help but be influenced by certain experiences. What I try to do is write out of some deep emotion about something. I'll hear something, or see something, or know something that touches some deep emotion that I've been feeling about any number of things, and that new awareness connects up with some older, deeper emotion, and my novels come out of that.

How did you come up with the idea of your second novel, Where You Once Belonged?

It's difficult to remember, but it started with the short story "Private Debts, Public Holdings," where Jesse Burdette is dancing at the Legion hall, and dances so much she loses her baby. It's a kind of sacrifice to the community.

Certain characters recur in your novels. Is there a conscious re-creation of them, or is it just the type of person that grows out of the story you're trying to tell?

It seems to grow out of the story I'm trying to tell, but there are similarities between the narrators of each book. I'm interested in men who are decent people and who're flawed, but still trying to do the best they can, but don't always succeed. In fact, they don't often succeed.

After you finished your second novel, you felt a kind of despair over it not being as good as you wanted it to be. Why did you feel that way?

That book should have been a lot better than it was. It should have been longer and more fully developed. I wrote it under pretty difficult circumstances and I was on contract to turn it in. I had to start teaching again, and I knew I wouldn't have time to write. So I forced myself to write it as fast as I could to get it done.

Some people have compared Plainsong *to the work of Cormac McCarthy. Are there any similiarities?*

Only superficial ones. Some people point to the fact that this book doesn't have quotation marks, and of course Cormac McCarthy doesn't either, but he's not the only one. There are other contemporary writers who don't use them. People also point out that this book is set in the West, just as his most recent books are. Some think I use the word *and* in the way he does, although I don't think so. But I think it's not very deep thinking to say that *Plainsong* is like Cormac McCarthy's work. It's flattering, of course, but Cormac McCarthy is the greatest living American writer. He's head and shoulders above most of us. But I can't see that my fiction is very much like his.

Why did you disregard the rules of grammar like quotation marks and question marks?

When I wrote *The Tie that Binds* in manuscript that book had no quotation marks, so it was something I'd been thinking about for a long time. I changed my mind when I sent that book off to the agent and publisher, and I put quotation marks in. I've been thinking about quotation marks to some degree since I'd read Faulkner in such books as *The Bear* and *The Sound and the Fury*, which have passages without quotation marks. And I like the way it looked on the page, and it seemed appropriate and arresting. So part of my defense of not using quotation marks in *Plainsong* is that I like the way it looks on the page. I'd also like to think that quotation marks are just another convention in the writing of prose, and if you can violate that convention and still make your prose understandable, and it's clear that dialogue is different from exposition or straight narration, then it's all right. It also breaks down the arbitrary separation between dialogue and exposition. When people say things or make remarks that are questions, they're not really questions at all sometimes, but a kind of flat statement. One way of indicating that in dialogue is not to use question marks.

Is there a difference in style between Plainsong *and your other books?*

Yes, there is some difference. The books are similar, but this last book seems more pared down and cleaner and more direct. I never give any of the thought processes of these characters. My intent is to simply present them in some external way and see them and know them from what they say and do. Just as we see and know most people we come into contact with. That's about all we do know about them. And if you pay attention, you can know a great deal by gestures and by what they say and how they act, even if you don't know what they're thinking.

Two of the most original characters in Plainsong *are the McPheron brothers. How did you come up with them?*

The germ for those two guys came out of my acquaintance with two old bachelor, farmer brothers who lived out in rural Colorado. They came to my father's church every Sunday in their black suits and white shirts. They were very shy, and I don't remember them ever saying anything. But I had those two old men and that situation in my mind for fifty years.

Another important center of the book is Tom Guthrie and his two sons, who seem like they could have come out of your own background.

Tom Guthrie and the two boys came out of the short story that I wrote back in the eighties about the autopsy of a horse, and that scene gets into this novel. But that man and those two boys—and that relationship and what becomes of the mother of that family—all originated in that story. So I'd been thinking about those two boys and that father for fifteen years or more.

The scene of the horse autopsy is realistic in detail, and you mentioned that it came from one of your own experiences.

That was an event that I witnessed when I was visiting my brother on his ranch in Colorado. He had a cowboy named Snuffy Drummond who was one of the best cowboys in that part of Colorado. One of Snuffy's horses died, a good expensive roping horse. I happened to be there the morning the horse died, and the vet came to perform an autopsy to see what killed it. He cut the horse open and examined the entrails in the way I described, and afterwards sewed it back up. So when I got home I made notes of what I'd seen, thinking that someday that might be a good piece of fiction.

After exposing Tom Guthrie's boys to the theme of death with the autopsy scene, why was it necessary to repeat it when they found Ida Stearns dead?

The boys are put through a series of experiences which initiate them into the harsh world of adults. Earlier on in the book they witness some raw sexuality, and then they witness the autopsy of a horse, and then they see the death of the old woman. So there's a kind of progression and attempt to have a whole range of experiences which lead them to a kind of exposure to human and adult reality.

Maggie Jones acts as a catalyst among the characters in the story, and she's a connector between people. Did the story come to need her as you wrote it, or did you visualize her from the beginning?

She was in the story from the beginning. She's the one who knows all of them. She's the one person who changes the least in the course of this novel. She's a complex, mature, wise, healthy woman, and straight talking, and she sees through people, but she's extraordinarily generous and warm at heart.

But all the other characters do change and mature by the end of the book.

Yes, they all have changed somewhat and progressed in some way, and perhaps they're all coming up to Maggie Jones's level.

Did you consciously try to decrease the violence in Plainsong *compared to your other books?*

I tried to write a novel that was still compelling without being driven by violence or unnecessary sexuality. I was trying to write a story in which ordinary people living ordinary lives were trying to find ways to deal with their problems, and yet still give this novel enough momentum that people wanted to turn pages to see how it turned out. I didn't intend to write a story that depended on violence to make it seem compelling.

You use a lot of detail about ranch life in all your books. Did this knowledge come out of experience or research?

I've seen a lot of cowboys and ranchers doctor cattle, and I've participated in that in a very menial way. I'm usually the guy out there in the dust trying to get the cattle to move into the chute. I pay close attention and take notes when I get home, so I do know something about it. I certainly want to be as accurate as I can and use the right terms, and to make these men speak in the right ways as they would in these circumstances. Occasionally I've checked with my older brother to make sure I was saying these things right and using the right details, but most of that is just recall of what I've seen.

Your books seem very connected. Are they a kind of High Plains trilogy, or part of a larger cycle?

I would never define them that way. They're very separate because there're few characters who reappear in each book.

Will you ever exhaust writing about Colorado?

I think of that corner of Colorado as being my material. I feel like I own that in some literary sense. There's so much to write about there that I don't think I'll exhaust it. But I don't think of these stories as separate from the rest of the United States. What I do think is that I'm trying to tell stories that are pared down enough that the skeleton of human behavior can be seen where the distractions of the city are gone.

How did you come up with the title Plainsong?

When I sent this novel off to my agent and to Gary Fisketjon at Knopf, it had a very cumbersome title: *O, They Tell Me of an Unclouded Day*, which was a bluegrass song made popular by Willie Nelson. Obviously, that was too long. I was going through the dictionary one day to see what words were associated with *plain* or *plains*. Once I came to *plainsong* it seemed appropriate. It's a kind of pun for what I'm trying to do in this book, but it also has a kind of relevance in terms of its meaning. I'm trying to tell a story in some sort of un-adorned way, but in which there's a sense of unison where all the characters are singing at once.

When you finish a novel do you let anybody read it before you send it off to New York?

I will sometimes read aloud passages from a work-in-progress to my wife, even occasionally to students, but once I've gotten more than a third of the way into a book some-thing happens that I don't want to have anybody hear any more of it. Part of the danger of doing that is that people will say things well meaning, but even so, they say things that somehow have the wrong emphasis or put you off a while from what you're working on.

Once the book's done, do you let your wife read it?

I do let Cathy read the manuscript, and I have a couple other friends. I have Rodney Jones, the poet, and my good friend Richard Peterson, and a couple other people who're writers, just to see if I've done what I hoped to do. I'm not really looking for any critical attention or review, but simply trying to get some kind of literate response to it.

If someone came to you today and asked you how to become a successful novelist, what would you tell them?

First, you have to be a reader and to have read a good deal. You have to read with concentration and close attention to what's going on on the page, and to be open to the magic of what's happening, and be open to a kind of religious experience of literature that's essential. After that the thing to do is to write and write and write. It can't be said too emphatically that the way to learn how to write is to write. Then you have to be open to being instructed. Either by your own efforts or by other people. Perhaps the most important thing is to be persistent. Most people who have some inclination to write quit before they get good enough at it to get published because it's too difficult.

What books are you reading right now?

I've just finished reading the new biography that you wrote on Dylan Thomas, which corrected some misconceptions about Thomas. Recently, I read *Snow Falling on Cedars* and I've just started reading Cormac McCarthy's *The Crossing* for the second or third time.

When you finish a book, do you get postpartum depression?

I guess it's something like that. There's a kind of letdown. Somehow it has to do with the fact that you've been intensely involved with something for a number of years. Now that's over. So you're out of sorts, and you're not sure what do to with yourself.

Do you immediately start preparing for the next book or give yourself a break?

No, I feel I have to fill up again. There's a song a friend wrote called "Getting Back to the Well." I have to fill up again. I have to feel some emotional compulsion to write the next book, so I wait for that. I begin to make some notes about the next book, but I don't actively start writing for a while.

Do you think of yourself as a Western writer?

Only in the sense that I write stories set in the West. It irritates the hell out of me to think anything I write is regional literature. I don't believe that at all. Novels have to be set somewhere, and my novels are set in northeast Colorado because that's what I know. I want to think that what I'm writing about is universal and elemental so that it applies to people living anywhere.

What's the West's place in American history?

The West, in terms of mythology, is still thought of as a place where new beginnings are possible. Where there are fewer restrictions and fewer boundaries. Where you can go and live life in a more raw and elemental way. A lot of that is myth, but it's still current in American psychology.

Plainsong *has been hugely successful. You said you were glad success came to you late. Why was that?*

Good fortune and money and notoriety can be very dangerous and seductive if you're not mature enough to deal with them. I didn't have that problem. It's my contention that people in this country don't know how to deal with success. I'm not suggesting that I'm famous, and I don't want to be. We were talking about various writers who seemed to have written better things before they became famous. By the time this book came around and did well, I was certainly old enough to not be distracted by it. I keep telling people that I'm so old and my neck is so stiff that it won't turn my head.

Gary Fisketjon, your editor at Knopf, seems like an old-style

*editor, very hands-on, using a blue-pencil treatment on a book. You
mentioned that he went through the book two or three times.*

Gary read it first to decide if he wanted the book. Once he
began the editing process, he read it very carefully. He told me
one time that he'd read the book more carefully than anybody
except me, and I believe that. He went sentence by sentence
and made numerous marks, and asked numerous questions.
He says what he's doing is starting a conversation on the page
with me about what was written on the page. What he tries to
do as an editor is to make sure that the writer is up to the best
of his own standards.

*If you could give up teaching and write full time, would you like to
do that someday?*

Any writer would like to do that. I've enjoyed teaching, and
I've done a good job, and I've tried to be conscientious about
it. My ideal would be to write in the morning and then do
something physical in the afternoons. Some kind of physical
work like mending fences, stacking hay, or fishing or riding
horses or walking or hiking.

Who are some of your favorite characters in literature?

I like V.K. Ratliff in the Snopes saga by Faulkner, and Mink
Snopes. Mink is such a fierce and nasty, narrowly focused guy.
He's beset by all sorts of problems, and he finds his own nasty
way of dealing with them. I don't want to live next to him.
He's interesting from a distance.

*What is your biggest strength and your biggest weakness as a
writer?*

From my own point of view, I'd say I have some skill at
writing about characters who, in Faulkner's phrase, cast a
shadow and seem real. I have a fair ear for dialogue and
making characters speak in a realistic and accurate way. I have
a bit of skill in describing landscape and scenery. I've begun to
learn how to pace a novel. The flaws or weaknesses are that I
wish I had a more lyrical talent, but I don't seem to have that.

I'd like to be able to write in a lyrical vein, and to do what James Agee does in the beginning of *A Death in a Family* and in *Let Us Now Praise Famous Men*.

Mario Vargas Llosa said that he wrote because he was unhappy and that writing was a way of fighting unhappiness.

I do think you write out of your unhappiness, and out of pain and anguish. I don't think that fixes it or heals anything, but I feel very strongly that that's what a writer does.

H. G. Carroll

On a bus in Chicago—many, many miles and what seems to be centuries away from the where and the when of this moment— I met the man who had been the boy with whom I was placed on detention for shoving in line just before this picture was taken. It was he who recognized me, and he greeted me by slapping me on the back of the head and saying, Ay coño 'mano, you hardly no change at all, no? And because my initial impulse was to knock him down, I have since assumed he was right.

H. G. Carroll lives and teaches in Ithaca, New York, where he is an MFA/ PhD candidate in the department of English at Cornell University. He is currently completing his first novel.

H. G. CARROLL
Leche

FIRST-PLACE WINNER
Fiction Open

*B*etween the sweet distraction of a hangover and the ache of waking, the abuelo who Arnulfo Mendoza has never met—only seen in pictures—towers over him, holding the babies. A great, inky arm wrapped around each—Oné y Tomas o Luis y Carlos—Arnulfo can see the light-brown pingas y rosy huevitos curled and exposed like shelled snails between their thighs. Through the dark sky behind them, he sees the palmas reales near Guantánamo Bay. He remembers their fronds swaying black and white at the end of his own father's finger in the stilled breezes of a photo album where his tío Ernesto, with the fierce, wide grin, stood holding the longest bacalao anyone could remember; and Ernesto's wife, tía Juanita, and their four daughters, all named Ernestina—Ernestina-María, Ernestina-Luisa, Ernestina-Teresa, Ernestina-Gabriela—arranged in order of height in front of the

Glimmer Train Stories, Issue 42, Spring 2002
©*2002 H. G. Carroll*

little blue house close to the shore where Arnulfo's father and his father's father and his father's father's father stood with the pride of ownership back for as long as could be recalled.

¡Mira! his abuelo calls as he lets go. And, instinctively, Arnulfo reaches for his shirttails to catch the babies as they spill above the leathery fronds of the palmas calling, Papi, Papi, Papi, in the blackness beyond his reach.

He opens his eyes to the smell of bacon coming from the townhouse next door. Arnulfo believes the man's name is Magnusson, but he isn't sure. They met once a few months back. Now they wave. Arnulfo watches him when he isn't looking. The man is blond, pink-skinned, a lawyer; his wife kisses him full on the mouth, and his daughter clings to his pant leg each morning at the front door before he leaves for work.

The sheets are soaked through, and, as Arnulfo carries them to the hamper, he sees his wife sitting at the kitchen table waiting for the kettle to boil. Alicia has put away the pillow and blankets she now uses to make the couch her bed. She has picked up the clothes he left in the hallway and the living room last night.

At the bottom of a cup, a teaspoon of freeze-dried coffee holds her attention. Alicia bundles her bathrobe around her. Slumped forward in the chair, her heavy black hair falls over her face and covers her eyes. As the kettle begins to hiss, she decides she'll wait until its whistle screeches bloody murder before she moves. She tries not to think of wind or ice or cold or the thin blanket of midwestern snow covering everything outside the window before her.

Her eyes shut to the sound of the shower, and eventually she hones in on the padding of her husband's feet against the tile, his razor tapping against the sink. He slaps aftershave into his cheeks, and ruffles his back with a towel that she knows he'll leave on the floor between the toilet and the tub. She is unsure if the wailing she hears comes from inside her head or from deep in her heart, and goes out through her fingertips, her toes, her vagina, her mouth. She has no idea the water is boiling until her husband turns the kettle off.

Without opening her eyes she knows he has wrapped her towel around his waist. The tightly curled black mat of hair on his chest glistens from the shower and there is shaving cream behind his ears. She tracks his presence through the light vibrations he makes as he pours water into her cup, empties more than a teaspoon of coffee into a mug for himself, and leaves the open jar on the counter and the lid on the table in front of him. There is a pause between the scrape of his chair against the black and white tiles and the slurp and grunt of his first sip.

She knows he has stirred the cup with his index finger and wiped it off on her towel. And she scrunches her eyes to suppress a long-ago image of her using the hem of her nightgown on the backs of his ears. She pushes her tongue back in her mouth, safe from the temptation to taste where he is in need of a haircut at the nape of his neck. She keeps her eyes closed to the empty cupboards that line the kitchen walls and the two eggs that have been in the cardboard crate in the back of the refrigerator since long before she last looked in there. There is no cereal, no rice, no meat, no cheese. No forks, glasses, knives, or plates; no herbs or spices, no sugar. Arnulfo will take the four empty wine bottles that peek from the top of the garbage on his way out. They drink their coffee black.

Alicia avoids his eyes as she gets up from the table. Arnulfo knows she'll wash her cup—caressing it over and over with a kitchen sponge she has soaked in nearly an eighth of a cup of dish soap—rinsing it with the water from the kettle before putting it into the dishwasher. He knows that as she is getting dressed—brushing her hair in the mirror, lipsticking her mouth a light orange—that she'll be listening for him to wash his cup, too. She'll wait until he's dressing before she'll put it on the rack next to hers and turn the machine on. He'll be tying his tie when she'll ask if he'll pick up a chicken or half a pot roast from the delicatessen on his way home, and he won't ask about a salad or vegetable or potatoes. He'll buy more wine.

And as she leaves for work, he imagines her at a time she enjoyed making him breakfast: huevos y frijoles negros; galletas light enough not to be there at all; his arms full of her, warm and fleshy like the girl he met whose mouth tasted hot and insistent; the girl who asked for his help opening and closing the clasp of her bra.

The door clicks and he can hear their two cups clinking in the whorl and slap of the water against the otherwise empty dishwasher. And it's a sound that she'll keep in her head as she turns on her car and as she scrapes the windows and removes the snow off of the roof. She'll hold onto it until she can arrange herself behind the wheel and can turn the radio loud enough so that news and the engine might drown out any noises the babies—Carlos y Tomas o Luis y Oné—might make as she turns out onto the boulevard to the freeway.

When she turns onto the exit ramp and merges toward the center lane, she no longer feels the low, heavy swish of them wash through as they had those months they were inside her. Nor did she imagine a groan they might have somehow inherited from Arnulfo: the one he made as he turned over in his sleep or getting up from a chair. The only voice she hears tells her there is more wind, more snow, more freezing rain on the way: When will this end, it chuckles from what Alicia imagines to be a very hairy chest. Just ahead of her, a grey light that seems in no way connected with the sun begins to fill in the sky between the downtown office buildings. Looking at the clock, she thinks of the work piled in her In-bin, the phone calls she needs to make, and the letters she'll need to sign as Head of Human Resources. She knows about this time Arnulfo should be turning his truck onto the freeway.

He's headed out of the city to an empty lot in the suburbs.

He knows he's there when the road narrows to a two-lane highway and he reaches what was part of the asphalt leading to a parking lot when a pharmaceuticals distributor stood there. His truck is new and red, and shimmers in places under a thin layer of ice despite the grey overcast light. His head sings a muffled throb and feels raw in the cold air as he wades chest-deep into a sea of dead weeds.

Toward the far end of the lot, where the road curves around and heads back toward the city, a sign tells of the coming of shops, fast food, and conveniences. Under his company's logo, Arnulfo's signature has been painted. Underneath it is the number he was assigned by the American Institute of Architects. The developer, his boss, and the client trust the number he was assigned. We trust Arnie, they say. So, if Arnulfo wants, he can have the cottonwood in the center of the lot removed tomorrow morning; a county surveyor and a refuse collection crew could be summoned to the site at his whim.

He wants to bring his mother-in-law to this place, and have her watch him will a drugstore into being, or create a shop where she can't resist trying on a pair of shoes or sampling a fragrance.

During the weeks she had visited after Alicia had come home from the hospital, his mother-in-law knitted or read or attended to Alicia as her daughter instructed. No matter how cold it was, if Alicia wanted to go for a walk, they walked. And Arnulfo watched from the window as the two women huddled through the snow and rounded the corner. If Alicia wanted lemon-grass tea with milk and honey, her mother would make and remake cup after cup until it was the right strength, the right sweetness, the right temperature. Alicia wanted there to be no cooking in the house. She had cried like a little girl catching her breath as she coughed out each sob, and her mother demanded that Arnulfo drive her to places where they made fríturas like she used to make, and a place where the arroz con pollo was seasoned with real saffron and not just dyed yellow like so many places up north liked to do, and a somewhere where the yucca was fresh and completely cleared of sand and grit. She instructed him to drive quickly without killing them so that she could get it home to Alicia while it was still steaming, while it could do her some good. As always she had seemed distant to him. Not a coolness, but he was very aware of a ten-year-old polite reserve between them that always made him feel as if he was meeting her for the first time whenever they were alone. Once, while he and his mother-in-law were in the car looking for the mafungo Alicia craved, saying she could eat nothing else, they had passed an apartment complex for which Arnulfo had designed the lobby. He explained how it had taken him nearly a year to come up with the right plan—one that fit the rest of the building, but was still distinctive—and how he had sweated during all the months of construction, not knowing how his vision would turn out. He asked his mother-in-law if she cared to stop and see it. ¿Por qué, the woman asked without turning to look at him, did you build it? Arnulfo, mijo, was there dirt under your fingernails after the earth was opened up and your ideas were poured into it? Besides, the food will get cold, she said.

He paces the steps between where the Midwest's Largest Fabric Emporium will go and a place where pretzels that taste like buttered cinnamon toast will be sold. Down the corridor where security will sit across from a discount beauty-supply store, Arnulfo unbuckles his belt, and pulls his trousers and shorts to the middle of his thighs. As he pushes an arc of urine out onto the exact spot where a firewall will

be raised, a station wagon passes on the road just in front of
him.

Despite the fact that the car is gone within seconds, he
waves as the sound of the tires against the road fades. The car
is headed south and Arnulfo is certain a young boy rides in the
far backseat; he wants there to have been an entire household
of goods and luggage strapped to the carrier on the roof, and
imagines the car traveling non-stop out of Chicago, out of
Illinois, through Indiana; he imagines it headed south, south,
south, until it reaches the Bay of Biscayne, and the backdoor
opens to a white expanse of beach with blue water and air,
and the beach ball the boy throws is a bright orange, as a
group of gulls picks through the sand, and sun plays on his
nose and shoulder blades.

The wind against Arnulfo's buttocks sends a rash of goose-
flesh up his back and down to his ankles. His genitals threaten
to crawl inside of him, although he holds on to his image of
the boy and the bright ball and the sound of the waves and the
squeals of gulls until he is blue to the quick.

In his truck with his shirt arranged in his trousers, he rubs
his thighs and smacks his shoulders in the blow of the heater
as he tries to regain feeling. He's the architect; We trust Arnie,
they say. He stomps his feet against the floorboards and presses
the speed-dial button that connects him to Alicia's office. He
listens to her outgoing message—she's back in the office; it's
unfortunate she's unable to take his call right now; she looks
forward to talking to him. Instead of leaving a message, he
hangs up and dials again. She's back; it's unfortunate; she looks
forward, and he hangs up without telling her about the crows
that, one by one, streak the sky overhead and grab hold of the
bare cottonwood with a screech so clear and distinct it pierces
the hum of the truck's engine.

However, it is a baby's screech across the marble lobby of
her office building that sets Alicia's body into motion.

H. G. Carroll

She has hung her coat and checked her In-bin. Her assistant's desk is empty, and the researchers have yet to make it in. The snow, she thinks. Qué weather, slowing down the trains and busses; the freeways will become full and still in another fifteen minutes.

The phone on her desk blinks. The machine forces her to listen to her outgoing first: She is back (now, for nearly a month after being gone for eleven weeks); unfortunately, she is unable to take your call. But she begins to wonder if she sounds contrite. She knows Arnulfo is the four dial tones in a row. She listens to them as if they are fugitive love songs, boleros of longing and loss; so tender, as if coming from an animal wounded by birth with a vital organ outside its body. When she thinks of him it is no longer of the smell of melon she would search and find in the center of his chest or the sinew of muscle across his back. Nor are the echoes of her girlfriends' whispers—Muy guapo; Y macho; So smart; Tan fuerte; Such a good provider; You're lucky—in her head. Now she thinks of the instant, constant, nervous cant that is his heart.

She would have played them over and over, but the last of them runs into a message thanking her for an interview she had the day before. The woman was pleased that she was able to meet with all the people on staff and looked forward to working there. The next message was from Mike, a researcher, reminding her that he will be late this morning. He has a dentist appointment.

Arnulfo had called at 2 A.M. to leave her his dial tone, and again twenty-three minutes later. Between them her mother said, Escucha, mija, if you want to know what all of downtown Habana smells like during the hottest of August afternoons, take an onion, garlic, the juice of one lime, and olive oil, and fry them in a pan until they become gritty and black as gravel…

Alicia interrupts her mother's message, and as soon as she hangs it up, her phone begins to ring. She lets the call go to voicemail.

The In-bin contains applications, resumes, and offers of solicitation from vendors. Her doctor's release to return to work is still there. For any other employee she would have approved it, signed it, and immediately had it filed.

In her mind, her mother is still the thin, tanned woman who raised her, even though she has gained weight and aged quite a bit. The messages, no matter what time of day or night, seem to come from a long-ago noon, poolside in back of the pink house in Miami where she grew up. Her mother's bikini matches the house. Tito, her mother's ancient green parrot whose only word is ¡Coño! marches around the lawn near the gazebo, and the water in the pool is blue, blue. She imagines her mother picking up the white princess phone to begin a story about a cousin in Holguín who ate nothing but wild pineapple for a year while she waited for her lover to come back to her. Alicia knows the story. She knows all of the stories: the tío with the coffee finca who had one arm and more mistresses than socks; or how the recipe that she uses to make picadillo came into the family, and the murder of a diplomat associated with it. She can see her mother check the hard helmet of black hair she kept up for so many years, even though the last time Alicia saw it in the hospital when the babies—Carlos, Oné, Tomas, Luis—seemed so present, so real, her mother's hair was wild and frazzled and streaked with grey.

The phone begins to ring again. Alicia lays the release aside and takes the elevator to the lobby to get a bagel and a cup of coffee.

She is standing in line when she hears the baby screech. The woman in front of her turns in the direction of the baby—she sees a woman negotiating a stroller covered with a pink and yellow blanket through the revolving door into the brightly lit lobby—but Alicia fixes her eyes on the menu above the counter. She notes the prices of scones with currants, scones with blueberries, and scones with raspberries have gone up in the last month, when the woman removes the blanket, and the baby, shocked and red in the sudden light, begins to bawl.

It is an angry, hungry cry, a repeating bleat from quavering lips that resounds in the lobby and stiffens Alicia's spine, causing her to abandon her place in line and make her way to the washroom with her purse over her chest.

In the stall, she checks for spots before unbuttoning her blouse and unclasping her bra. Milk seeps through her fingers as she uses the other hand to fish in her purse for the pump. She watches as it is expressed from her body, and curls down the plastic tube into the container she will rinse and dry before returning it to her purse and taking the elevator back to her office. During a break, she'll find a message from her mother; in the background she'll hear Tito yelling ¡Coño! ¡Coño! ¡Coño! And around lunchtime, Arnulfo will call to hear her voice: she's back; it's unfortunate; she looks forward.

It is after lunch that Arnulfo returns to his office and discovers that he has been entrusted with the design of a closet that is both decorative and functional. The developer, a squat hairy man who appears to be sweating even when he's not, says they are counting on him. We know you'll make it good, Arnie, he says.

Arnulfo stares at the linen paper stretched out on his drafting table waiting for the closet to appear. He balances the point of his mechanical pencil with his index finger in one of the dimples on the clean sheet in front of him. The pocket clip catches his fingernail, sending the pencil flying out of sight. As he is on his hands and knees looking for it, he can hear two women outside his office discussing plans for a coworker's birthday. There will be balloons and a gift certificate; cake from the bakery down the street, they'll begin passing the card around in the morning. He returns to his seat empty handed. The thin trail the pencil left stops at the end of the page.

There was a time he could place a single line on the center of the page and with confidence whisper, Mira, Alicia, una silla. And he wouldn't stop until she could see it, could name the texture and color of the fabric, the type of wood frame that supported the full cushion that she would sink into as she read by the fire. Mira, Alicia, una ventana, he'd whisper. And she would tell him about the cat—an Abyssinian, she was certain—that she would go after with a bucket of water every afternoon until it stopped lying in wait in the hedgerows to dig up the bulbs she planted. She promised peonies as large as cabbages and cabbages bigger than any cabbage that he'd ever seen.

And when all the floors had been sanded and the dust cleared, they stood in the empty, finished townhouse and he said, Mira, Alicia, tu casa. And she knew what color the walls would be, and which rugs went where, and what would have to be bought, and what they shouldn't bring with them. She knew she was working against time. Mira, Alicia, Arnulfo had whispered, as her doctor pointed to arms and legs and fingers and scrotums through the shadowy float of an ultrasound.

She is nearly the last person left in the office. Through the windows that line the entire floor, she is too high up and it is too dark to tell if it is still snowing. Cars on the freeway in the distance seem to be moving slowly.

As she files her medical release she notices the light blinking on her phone. She listens to the dial tone blare and fade, and then Tito screeches ¡Coño! Her mother wants to know if Alicia remembers her great tía Adele's hair. Yards and yards of it there was; a strange color of dark red that no one else in the family had or has had since. And when her mother was a girl in La Habana, she and her sisters would have to cover the dining-room table with a cloth and spread it out to be cleaned with arrowroot, anise, and lavender root. Not fond of water she was, your great tía, her mother says. But how you loved her hair, even though you have only seen it through my eyes; you loved it without seeing, smelling it, touching it; you loved it.

In the elevator, Alicia adjusts her scarf and puts on her gloves. She makes a mental note of the things she needs to do the next day. In her In-bin are several applications, resumes, and offers of solicitation from vendors; most of her staff will be there; they will have a meeting to plan her day; interviewees will sit outside her office in dry-cleaned clothing and shoes they've tried to preserve from the salt and slush.

She's looking for her car keys when the elevator stops between the third and fourth floors. Waiting in the dim light, she knows that it won't be long before the maintenance people load the dumpster from the floor above onto the freight elevator. She hums one of Arnulfo's boleros—one of the ones he used to sing upon waking, going to bed, in the shower, in the car, so out of tune she could almost not bear it—over and over to herself, as if she were testing a bad tooth with her tongue. One day, she will be able to hand him a piece of paper and a pencil and say, Una silla, por favor. One day, they'll take their things out of storage and she'll paint one of the garden walls cobalt, and grow yellow clematis over it. She'll keep oranges out on the counter until they are hot with that nearly fermented flavor that is so warm and sweet. She would, one day, look at Arnulfo as he read the newspaper Sunday afternoons at the kitchen table and crumpled peanut shells onto the floor, and think, Tan fuerte, muy guapo. They'd fill the refrigerator with savory and favored tastes; their kitchen would always smell of cooking. And she is as certain as she knows the elevator doors will open, her car will start, she will make her way home through the traffic and the snow, and find Arnulfo there. Certain as she was standing there, she

knows that between the two of them, each has kept an island—one neither of them has ever seen, touched, or
smelled—poised from the time they were born for just this
moment now. Although what frightens, more than anything,
is the rocking of the dim elevator car, pendulous on its cable,
so reminiscent of the babies—Oné y Tomas o Luis y Carlos—
falling out of her over and over again. When will the feeling
not leave her chilled and shivering?

She thinks of a blue house just beyond Guantánamo Bay,
and plátanos rojos and the summer nights her tíos would burn
tarántula nests from the trees, and of palmas reales near a
beach so white and water so blue.

Before she gets home, Arnulfo turns the thermostat to
seventy-five. He has unwrapped the chicken and is opening a
bottle of wine when she comes through the door.

They sit in the dark in their coats at the kitchen table
passing the bottle between them. Outside, the moon makes
everything in the nearly empty rooms dark purple. If there is
wind they do not mention it. If there is more sleet, snow, or
frost predicted, neither admits to listening to a weather station
on the way home, or to a youth wailing about his angst, or a
diva crying about her abandonment, on a rock or from a
dungeon. Alicia scratches at nothing on the table with her
nail. Arnulfo runs the edge of his shoe on the thin lines made
between the black and white tiles.

As they finish the bottle of wine they listen to the child next
door confront bedtime. No, no, no, no, no, no, no, the baby
says as its mother cajoles with a singsong, Night-night. No, no,
no, no, no, she says, as she runs away from the wall that divides
the houses, until her hard, first shoes can no longer be heard
against the bare floorboards.

With his penknife, Arnulfo cuts portions away from the
breast of the chicken and lays the ragged slices on the paper bag
it came in, and pushes it in front of his wife. No, no, no, no, no,

the baby squeals with delight, as the room warms around them. Alicia removes her coat and opens another bottle of wine. No,

no, no, no, the baby says as the light through the window slowly shifts, and Alicia begins to see Arnulfo as he uses the lid from the macaroni salad container as a utensil. He has taken off his coat along with his tie and shirt. In the shadows, she watches a wash of sweat bead on his forehead and upper lip. His fingers fumble to find the chicken he left in front of her and hand her a piece. No, no, no, the baby says, as he tilts his head toward her, and listens to make sure she is eating. He brings carrot sticks toward her lips, a stalk of broccoli.

60

Night-night, and again, Night-night. They listen to the baby's feet running across the floors next door. Alicia takes the wine bottle from him and drinks deeply. Close to the wall and then away; little steps, unshod; in socks or pajamas that have feet in them. Alicia has seen them come in pink and blue and yellow and green pastels. Some have duck appliqués, others have bunnies; some come with mobiles to match.

Arnulfo has his shoes off, too. No, no, no, no, no, the baby says, and Alicia watches her husband take the garbage to the wastebasket, and listens as he pads about the kitchen in stocking feet; washing his hands; drying them on the towel in the handle of the refrigerator. On his way to retrieving a fresh bottle of wine, he undoes his belt and allows his trousers to fall to his ankles. He steps out of his socks, and removes his T-shirt. The languidness of his movements is infectious and familiar, like dancing. As she sees his legs and arms moving toward her, her body remembers wanting him to ask her to dance; she remembers being perched on the end of a wooden folding chair; remembers pretending to admire the decorations in the hall and trying to look deep in conversation with a girlfriend.

He stands in his underwear and offers her the bottle. ¿Qué calor esta noche, no, señora? he asks her. And she responds, Sí, señor. Do you know this beach well? he asks. And she tells him it has been in her family for thousands of years and she knows of a place where the water is so calm that he could be fooled into believing that there are two moons.

You'll show it to me, he asks.

She tells him, Momentito. Asks him to avert his eyes, and removes her clothes. She is standing barefoot in her underwear.

She takes his arm and leads him in front of the couch where the moon shines in the polish of the bare floors. She takes a sip of wine and unfastens her bra.

H. G. CARROLL

And for the few minutes he lies curled in her lap, the house where they live is quiet. And she whispers, Mira, this is the cove where afternoons swell with the most dizzying daylight. We'll like it here one day, she says. After all, it is happy.

FICTION OPEN
1st-, 2nd-, and 3rd-Place Winners

First-place winner: H. G. CARROLL

H. G. Carroll receives $2000 for his first-place story, "Leche," which begins on page 47, preceded by his profile on page 46.

Second-place winner: MALENA WATROUS

Malena Watrous receives $500 for "Gomi." She spent the past two years in Japan, teaching and writing essays that were published on Salon.com *and in* Kyoto Journal. *Before that she was a food critic for* Time Out New York. *She has an upcoming story in the* Alaska Quarterly Review *and is currently finishing her second year at the Iowa Writers' Workshop.*

Malena Watrous
"Gomi"

"Americans talk like cats," Miyoshi-sensei said. "Mrow, mrow, mrow." I began spacing consonants with hard Japanese vowels, slowing my speech until it seemed like my brain was slowing down, like I could never predict what word would follow the last.

Third-place winner: HESTER KAPLAN

Hester Kaplan receives $300 for "Companion Animal." Her fiction has appeared in many publications including The Best American Short Stories. *She is the author of* The Edge of Marriage, *which won the Flannery O'Connor Award for Short Fiction, and* Kinship Theory, *a novel published this year.*

Hester Kaplan
"Companion Animal"

He had been sure the weekend would deliver a word from her, a change of heart, but it hadn't, and he felt slightly beaten for having confused wanting something for believing it would happen.

We invite you to our website (www.glimmertrain.com) to see a listing of the top twenty-five winners and finalists. We thank all entrants for sending in their work.

J. M. Ferguson, Jr.

*Me holding tight to Black Jack, the first of the two
canine companions of my childhood and youth.*

A former traveling salesman but now mostly retired, J. M. Ferguson, Jr. lives
in Salem, Oregon, with his wife Holly, a former astrogeologist, and their
good friend Dilsey, mostly beagle. *The Summerfield Stories* was a first collection from TCU Press in 1985, and a second collection has been looking for
a publisher.

J. M. FERGUSON, JR.
Gleanings

A t the top of the first stone buttress which supports the wall of the church, it appears to Graves that the cement-cast gargoyle is missing, although, because it would be at the end of a row of them, this is not immediately clear. When he walks by in the early mornings he looks first for the pigeons which are often congregating on the crest of the pitched slate roof to catch the new sunlight, heedless of the aberrant inventions of humankind not far beneath them. Sadly, Graves can see that one of their number, ruffled and muddied, lies dead at the curbing. Their chorus of moans, mounting at intervals to a lugubrious chant, seems fitting, while the gargoyles, with folded wings and heedless in turn, extend their sleek necks and heads to gaze at the street below in mindless delight.

Except for Graves the street is deserted. In summer, though the Church of the Nativity is no longer in use, it is not unusual for him to see visiting tourists appraising the premises with camera in hand. Sensing that he must belong to the small western city he walks, they will sometimes ask him for directions, which he is always pleased to give. A former salesman who once traveled widely, and yet a loner all his life, he asks nothing more of his remaining years than peace and quiet; but even when both elude him, he finds he can still take heart in the smallest gestures of goodwill and civility.

Glimmer Train Stories, Issue 42, Spring 2002
©*2002 J. M. Ferguson, Jr.*

J. M. Ferguson, Jr.

Now at summer's end the prevailing quiet is only deepened by the mourning pigeons, and yet Graves has reason to distrust his hearing. He lives just a block, as the crow flies, from a large high school, and each fall he is entertained, like it or not—and Graves tries hard to like it—by the brassy blare of a marching band as they practice close by but out of sight on the school's football field. Possibly it has been a phenomenon prompted by just such circumstances, but during the summer something quite remarkable was occurring, causing him to pause, cock his head slightly, and listen intently. He could not be sure, but it sounded like the music of a band that he was hearing, a marching band, though out of season, and marching in his direction, too, for the sound seemed always to swell in volume while he listened.

His perceptions could at first be easily enough explained, being attributable to nothing more than the emanations from some downtown festivity, on which occasions, perhaps two or three times a summer, amateur bands did indeed play and sometimes parade to entertain the city's visitors. Yet as the summer progressed, Graves found the experience recurring at least weekly. Moreover, the music that reached his hearing seemed sublime. He could only conclude that the band he heard played not only with inordinate skill but with their whole hearts, for their renditions were truly arousing, beginning always faintly but carefully building to the most compelling crescendos, and eventually bringing him to his curb to peer down the long block he lived on to where it seemed the source of this enchantment was about to round the corner and come marching up the street to him.

But always the wonderful sounds stopped short, and the band, if there was one, never appeared. Graves was left to assume that he suffered from auditory illusions, though the possibility failed to disquiet him. With school resumed, he now listens again to the real band as it rehearses on the nearby field. The illusions have ceased, and, though still distrustful, he gives them no further thought.

Early in October, when Graves first sights the man, he is perched on his stool at the window of the Station House, having his morning coffee and just finding his place in the book he carries. Distracted, he glances up to see a well-dressed man in a light topcoat, British tan, and a derby hat—a professional of some sort, he infers, but someone he has never noticed before. He gives him no further thought until he arrives again from the direction in which he has passed, but this time he pauses to scan the sidewalk up and down, then studies the far side of the street as if seeking an address, or perhaps merely trying to get his bearings. Graves has a good look at him. He sees an unassertive mustache, well kept and greying, a neatly knotted tie, and, in the band of the derby, a modest little feather. Tall and rather slender, the man looks to be about the same age as Graves, who is sixty-seven. When he turns and begins to walk away, dropping his gaze, Graves can see that his chin is slightly receded and his cheeks a little hollow. His eyes look pale and forlorn, and his whole demeanor is that of a man given to indecision and introspection.

After this first encounter days go by before Graves sees the man again, but throughout the fall, as the days turn gradually colder, he keeps appearing at random until Graves begins to watch for him. As he makes his morning treks to the Station House, the man has a way of appearing in his vision at one point or another, perhaps well in front of him on the sidewalk or passing on the opposite side of the street, always in the tan topcoat, perhaps with a lining now buttoned into it to judge from the heavier way it has begun to enclose him. Once in a while he is hatless, as if the derby has been forgotten, but he has taken to wearing an expensive-looking pair of brown leather gloves. Pausing, as he is still wont to do, he will let his hands dangle as if from the weight of them, hesitate, then give his arms a little penguin-like flap against the slightly increased bulk of his coat, and make his worried way in the opposite direction.

Aside from the tourists, there are also the transients to be observed on the streets, especially in summer, but also in the fall while the weather holds. One morning when Graves arrives, one of them is seated in the Station House, wearing a heavy cableknit sweater, soiled and frayed, mumbling incoherently to anyone who will listen—Graves is able to catch accusatory phrases about a war somewhere and, surprisingly, about "the disappearing middle class." His hair matted and his face flushed, he keeps standing up beside his stool and holding aloft various coins which he fishes from the pockets of his greasy Levis, turning slowly as though inviting all to observe, and giving Chad, the young counterman, cause for concern.

Graves leaves before witnessing the outcome, but he knows it is not unusual for such drifting personages to hang around for days before disappearing, their unwelcome presence perceived as a threat and strained contrast to that of the summer vacationers who dine at their leisure in the best restaurants and out on the open patios. Their few possessions, if any, are packed on their backs or toted in plastic sacks which serve as makeshift luggage. Sometimes they travel in pairs and gabble at one another, but Graves has come to suspect that such pairings are also makeshift and the gabblers themselves transitory. More often they wander alone, though he has noticed that this does not necessarily inhibit the tendency toward conversation, whether with themselves or the world at large, which often as not rises to an argumentative pitch.

Graves wonders whether the solitary older man he is now always watching for could be one of them. Probably not, he reasons, for his gentlemanly appearance sets him apart, and perhaps even more telling, there is that touch of anxiety in his erratic wanderings which reminds Graves of a lost dog.

Then, glancing back while he walks in a November dawn, he perceives that the man is not far behind him—within earshot, surely, for he feels his disappointment as he overhears the threads of a conversation in progress. Still, he consoles himself with the observation that the monologue is not unseemly, the words, as far as he can discern, are free from profanity and incrimination, the volume controlled. Graves, for his own part, must admit that he occasionally catches himself enunciating some word or phrase aloud when alone.

He has finished his coffee and turned his first corner on the way home when suddenly he beholds the man again, this time loitering on the corner at the end of the block. But no, it is wrong to think he loiters, for he seems possessed again by that vague anxiety, hesitant, twirling his coat as he surveys his alternatives before striking out again, lifting a hand to the rim of his derby to shade his eyes as he turns them east toward Graves. While he is closing the space between them, Graves realizes they are about to pass on the same side of the street, for the object of his attention has begun to amble in his direction.

Intuitively, Graves knows better than to look too soon directly at the man, for he senses something fragile about him—not shyness, exactly, but something elusive, a propensity for avoiding further contact, perhaps, if approached too abruptly. He tries to appear nonchalant, but, just as they meet, with all the care that he can summon, he looks into the passing face and pronounces his "Good morning," extending what he hopes is all good will and warmth in the early morning sunlight. The man's glance slides across his own, registering for just the briefest instant, he thinks, consternation, but in the same instant recovering to offer the faintest of smiles, and even to nod. As seems his habit, he drops his countenance and passes without a hitch in stride, yet not before Graves has detected a soft but clearly spoken "Morning," which then resounds over and again to him as he makes his way homeward. Although he cannot be sure, he is tempted to believe that this fortuitous exchange has been the result of something other than mere chance.

"Little shits shouldn't be allowed to drive a car, if that's the best they can do with it."

His neighbor, fetching his morning paper, is trying to make conversation with him as Graves passes by, and he refers to the raucous rap of the teenagers who cruise this street near the high school with their radios throbbing, as one of them just has, even before the sun is up. Graves understands the man's annoyance.

He offers a tentative nod, smiling, but in truth he is not really sure what to make of it. He could move, of course. He has been down to Phoenix and Tucson and seen the various Sun Cities to be had there. Yet in the early mornings he passes the school parking lot and sometimes exchanges a greeting with the first of the arriving teachers, for whom he has come to hold unspoken respect, and he has decided to stay where he is. He tries instead to understand. Perhaps the urgent diatribes let loose on the streets are the poetry otherwise missing from their lives, and from what he can make of them they invariably take the form of protest. He should be encouraged, he knows, for it seems to him there is much to protest. Out on the interstates, back when he traveled for his living, he encountered epidemic speeding. He had gone so far as to construct a set of large white cards with bold black numbers—"65," "55," even a "45," for construction zones— and carried these reminders in the seat beside him, intending them for use on his fellow motorists. In the end, however, he thought better of it, and he never displayed them.

Now at the end of the block a youth in a souped-up low-rider careens around the corner, rubber squealing. He sees Graves staring, flips him a finger, and opens the throttle, doing what Graves takes to be a hundred down the street. Graves hopes he doesn't kill someone, or someone's dog. He recalls a dog he once observed in Phoenix, some years ago, when headed home in the roiling traffic of the urban freeway. It was midsummer, and in the scant shade of some portable concrete barriers left along the median, something caught his eye. Turning to look, he saw a stray dog, mistaking him at first for a coyote—which he resembled, save for his darker and brindled coloring. Reclining against a barrier in the cramped safety zone of the median, he lifted his head to stare calmly at nothing in particular, sphinx-like, while the traffic raged around him. It occurred to Graves to ease over and stop, to find somehow a break in the traffic and cross to the median, if all of that were possible; but even then, he foresaw, there would be the difficulty in approaching a dog like that, taking refuge where he had, at home in the eye of the storm.

What a state the world is in, Graves thinks, and, in truth, again, he suspects he is witness to the beginnings of a vast and unnameable deterioration, the causes of which are no longer debated or railed about. Yet they are nothing he likes to dwell upon, for he cannot think how he has ever raised a hand against them.

It is that same morning that Graves, seated in the hole-in-the-wall Station House, feels himself making his first mistake with regard to the newcomer who has taken to pacing the streets where he himself indulges in his daily walks.

"There stands our newest citizen," he announces to Chad, who is straightening some stools beside him at the window. The words slip out as if he were thinking aloud, and yet he continues, if only by way of explanation to Chad, who now

J. M. FERGUSON, JR.

stands watching. With a nod he indicates the well-dressed
man in the tan overcoat standing opposite them across the
street, as if searching for address numbers on their side of the
passing traffic, but looking a little bewildered.

"I've been seeing him around. Fascinating character." Forc-
ing a smile, he adds, "He's a symbol of sorts, I suppose."

Chad smiles, too. "Vibes," he offers, and Graves senses the
cogency of this brief summation.

As they speak, the subject of their observations begins to
cross the street. Dodging traffic, glancing when he can toward
their window, he gains the near sidewalk and presents himself
before the framed glass door. Just as he extends an arm, however, he draws back as though unsure of himself, reconsiders,
then turns on his heels and disappears down the sidewalk.

To his quick regret Graves realizes that he and Chad, forgetting themselves along with another patron or two, were
staring at precisely the wrong moment. Something tells him
he should never have spoken aloud of his new friend. For
such is the manner in which Graves has begun to conceive of
this man who, he must concede, remains a stranger to him.
Now, he fears, he might be gone for good.

Two days pass which seem to confirm his premonition, but
during the next morning the man comes pacing by the
window of the Station House, just in the place where Graves
first glimpsed him. He almost misses him, for this time he is
not only bare headed, with hair slightly mussed in the breeze,
but armed only with a brown leather jacket against the cold.
His hands are thrust into his pockets, and his face is inclined
forward in that familiar attitude which betrays his perplexity.
Graves, a little surprised to notice how his heart has acceler-
ated, finishes his coffee and takes to the sidewalk behind him.

At the nearest intersection he can see that halfway up the
block, where the sidewalk is closed by a construction project,

his would-be acquaintance is standing alone, hands still in pockets, apparently considering his alternatives. Graves proceeds slowly and is careful not to stare. The man has turned to peruse the window of the department store beside them, and Graves must address his back.

"Good morning," he offers, in the friendliest voice he can summon.

The man turns, this time as if expecting him, responds again with his clearly spoken "Morning," allows his not unfriendly glance to slide quickly over Graves once more, and then seems to search the distance down the street with eyes that fix themselves just above Graves's shoulder.

"Can I buy you a cup of coffee?" Graves pursues.

The man glances briefly into his face again—this time, Graves thinks, with sadness and perhaps the faintest trace of gratitude showing—and then looks back down the street.

"I have to wait for someone," he explains, and then begins to retrace his steps away from the construction site.

"Some other time," Graves suggests, by way of parting.

On the long walk home he considers again the man's last words, which led him to assume that he was waiting for a ride, for someone to pick him up, but now it seems to Graves that this was never likely, for the man was always alone. Graves begins to realize there is something about him—the gaunt cheeks when he pauses to take his bearings, the eyes that search the distance as if with expectation—that reminds him of someone, but someone he cannot put his finger on, and in the midst of this reflection he realizes, too, with certain knowledge, that he will never see the man again.

During the ensuing months Graves keeps an eye out for the man, though he knows in his heart it is useless. More fruitful are the reveries he finds himself indulging in throughout the meditative days of winter. Strange, he sometimes thinks, the things the memory chooses to retain. In the year of his retirement, for instance, he joined an alumni tour and went ten days to western Ireland, and the incident which stood foremost in his memory, to be retained above all else, seemed surely odd and possibly even insignificant.

Almost everywhere one looked there seemed to be a castle or an abbey, most in some stage of ruin but a few of them restored, and each day they were bused to one or another of them from their accommodations in the small city of Ennis, in County Claire. He watched the surf breaking on ancient cliffs, wondered at the neatly maintained homes and farms in their green landscapes. And yet what absorbed him most were the people themselves, their good nature and kindliness; but sometimes, too, if he passed them walking alone on the sidewalks of Ennis or some other town, their faces seemed touched with some distant melancholy even as they smiled at him.

At the end of their final day, returning to the outskirts of Ennis, his gaze fell upon the solitary figure of a man in the street where it curved and descended slightly between trim row houses, and joined the thoroughfare where their bus was just then slowly passing. It was also the end of the summer, and the sun was almost done with what had been an overcast and drizzly day. But where the top of the street formed a part of the horizon, the sky was soft and momentarily luminous. The man was a good half-block away, but as he lifted his face to them, Graves still thought he could detect that faintly melancholy smile, and, for reasons he could not have explained, he identified with this man who strolled alone in the September twilight, knowing also in that same moment that whenever he recalled his first and probably only trip abroad this was the incident which would come first and last to his mind.

With the coming of winter Graves retrieves the battered wood and Plexiglas bird feeder from his shed and hangs it in the crab-apple tree just off the front porch. Close by, he leaves the brass wind chime hanging throughout the year, taking care to keep it untangled.

Often the days are still warm, and he likes to retire to his study where the door opens onto the porch, allowing him to observe the tree with its feeder and the thick privet hedge beyond. He sees sparrows, finches, a few pine siskins, and, smallest of all and arriving only in winter, hooded juncoes with white bands in their tail feathers. Occasionally, too, there are boisterous visits from Steller's jays, but of them all Graves is fondest of the sparrows, who seem content to winter in his hedges with their spontaneous comings and goings.

There is a magical hour late in the afternoons when they gather in the cover there and make their erratic sorties to the feeder and back, when their gentle whistlings and whirrings awake in him a sense of quiet elation while, from behind his screen door, he sits silently watching. They brake and hover at the feeder while the sun goes down behind the hedge, and there are frozen moments when the feathered workings of their wings and tails are transparent in the light. Graves thinks of angels, though he gives no more credence to such entities than he gives to the gargoyles whose representations are preserved for him on the walls of the church.

On New Year's Day the Station House is closed, but by noon, the day turning warm, Graves wanders out all the same to stroll downtown. He passes by the high-school football field, where a pick-up game of tag football is just under way. There are eight youths, four of them in blue jerseys, who look to be college age. Their voices are bright in the sunshine. Graves himself, however, retains little interest in such sport, and walks on by, but not before some fragment of a memory begins to stir.

J. M. FERGUSON, JR.

He was sitting with his mother, who was young and beautiful, in a car parked among a row of them at the end of such
a field. His father, who taught at one of the high schools and
also coached the football team, was not there with them.
There was a red team and a blue team, which only now and
then attracted his attention. If he stood up in the seat he could
see them scrimmage in the distance, but once (and this is the
part that jogs Graves's memory) they all seemed to be running toward the goal posts he and his mother were parked
behind, chasing the ball which bounded loose upon the turf,
and some of them came so close he could see their faces
beneath their helmets.

Then for a little while the two teams left the field, and
something wonderful began to happen (though this part, sadly,
Graves does not recall). There was music which was growing
louder—beautiful music, it seemed to him—and rows of people
in red uniforms with broad white straps across their chests
came marching toward them. His mother told him this was
the band, and they both got out and sat on the hood of the car
in order to see better. The band drew closer to them, their
music gaining volume, and out in front of them was the thing
that fascinated him most: a man, dressed all in gleaming white,
was leading them. He wore a tall white hat with a bill which
shaded his upturned face, and his knees pumped high as he
marched, while his white-gloved fist held something flashing
silver—a baton, his mother said—which he also pumped up
and down. But just as he neared the goal post he suddenly
halted, and immediately the band also halted and broke off
playing. He blew a blast on a whistle he brought to his lips
with his free hand, and they all turned abruptly around. Then
the leader pranced quickly through the waiting ranks until he
was in front of them again, whistled a second time, and they all
marched away back down the field, playing something new.
Their music died away and eventually stopped, and they all left

the field at the far end where they first assembled. The two teams came straggling back onto the field, and he thought he could just make out his father, whom his mother pointed out, walking briskly behind the blue team.

Later, after the game, he was standing in the seat between the two of them while his father drove, and in the backseat sat a player they were taking to his home, a player named Earl Canterbury (the name, if nothing more, might still come back to Graves if there were anyone left to speak it). His helmet was placed on the seat beside him, and his hands and neck, protruding from his blue jersey, looked thick and strong. His sandy hair was damp and plastered to his forehead, and there was blood on the side of his face. Glancing around at him, he was aware that this was someone his father liked and esteemed.

"Did he like the game?" his father asked of his mother.

"He loved the band," his mother replied. "And he thinks he wants to be a drum major."

His father turned his head to assess them both, then slowly smiled.

Wakeful at night, Graves considers whether he is a part of the disappearing middle class, and hears the lonely wailing of freight trains which pass through the darkened city. Is it age, he wonders, or his want of employment now which brings him to this heady awareness of his own aloneness? Then he is lulled by the softer sound of the wind chime not far removed from his window left ajar, or of tires on the pavement just beyond, sometimes splashing lightly in the rain which by morning will have turned to snow.

On certain mornings in January he might wake to find his shrubs and hedges bent under the heavy whiteness, a branch from the silver maple already broken by the weight. Snow might still be falling and swirling, and the tops of the tall bare poplars behind his neighbor's home across the street still tossing in the unsettled air. There will be beauty in the scene beyond his window, yet he will not look forward to the wintry walk that awaits him. All the same, he will bundle up and go, taking care to wear shoes with good traction. His feet have more than once gone out from under him in such conditions, but he has learned to take his time and glance occasionally toward the mountains behind him. They might be veiled in snow and cloud, and when he gets downhill as far as the church they will be hidden from view, but he can be reasonably sure they are there, whether he sees them or not.

By February there are days which promise the spring, intermittent days when he wakes to the good will of a robin, perched somewhere in the still barren trees in his yard, singing in the dawn. Every year, it seems he tends to forget there will be such mornings, and always the first such occurrence is both new and familiar. He will rise and walk and from blocks away he will hear the piercing call of the flickers, who have stayed through the winter, he knows, but who choose to announce their presence only on such mornings as these. Such mornings as these, Graves reflects, when the air in his room with the window ajar is imbued with warmth and light and the cheer of birdsong.

Early in the morning on the third day of spring, Graves sights a dog running loose in the street up ahead. Tan with black markings, middle-sized, it summons to memory a dog from his boyhood. It disappears, but then it is back, closer now and pacing at an anxious trot. Like the dog he remembers, it is a short-haired male of obviously mixed breed, and the tips of the ears flop forward. Obviously, too, the dog is lost or abandoned. Spotting Graves alone on the sidewalk, he falls in behind him and begins to follow—Graves is familiar with the maneuver, other dogs having followed him in like manner. He thinks better of offering encouragement and walks steadily on, but the dog trots faithfully at his heels as though trying to pass himself off as a friend of long standing.

They are soon downtown together, but just as they near the Station House the dog is distracted by a pigeon foraging at the curbing close by. He gives chase just as Graves is entering. Perched on his stool at the plate-glass window, Graves can see his erstwhile companion pacing anxiously in the street once more—looking for him, he knows.

But the dog has vanished, to his relief, by the time he gets up to leave. Still, his relief is not uncomplicated. It is the beginning of his sixty-ninth year, as it happens, and he has declined this offer of friendship—from a would-be friend, moreover, who reminds him of one long ago. In the mornings that follow he looks in vain for him, and at the end of a week he determines he will drive out to the animal shelter, on the far side of town, for a look around.

Graves has never visited a prison, yet on his visit to the animal shelter he feels immediate empathy with the impounded dogs—something like a déjà vu experience, he considers, though he has never before had occasion to take the concept seriously. There is even a metal door which slams behind him as he enters the area where four rows of cages, some forty-eight of them altogether, await his inspection.

Hesitantly, he makes his way before them, attempting to avoid contact for too long with eyes that beseech him, though some are not without suspicion and fear, or even rage—one dog, seemingly almost feral, leaps at the door of his cage to get at him as he passes. Yet near the end of his tour his gaze alights on a sight which gives him pause. Trembling and cowed in the shadows at the back of its cell, there stands an animal looking so despondent that he fears for its survival—a young female shepherd mix, a nameless stray according to the card on her cage, perhaps part greyhound or whippet, he thinks, to judge by her thinness. For just a moment she returns his gaze, revealing eyes not so much pleading as deeply hurt, but then she quickly averts them, allowing them to close as she lowers her head, and Graves is stung to the heart by the gesture.

So it is that Graves, seeking one dog without success but in the process stumbling upon another, is back at the pound in another day, yet only to discover, as the heavy door slams shut behind him once again, that the cage he seeks is now deserted.

"It's a shame, but we have to do it," the attendant out in the lobby informs him. "We just don't have room for everybody." While Graves is reflecting on this usage of "everybody," the man attempts a further justification. "When they're sick and obviously not going to make it. Sometimes also if they're mean and aggressive." The dog that leaped and lunged at Graves is also gone.

Then, while standing outside in the open air, he notices that four or five youths who have arrived in a church van are now walking some of the dogs, and it occurs to him that all of this was somehow meant to be. He completes the necessary form for volunteering, and he soon finds himself wandering the wooded hills outside the pound with a grateful dog on the end of his leash. He also finds that by arriving at opening hour, nine in the morning, he has time to take out three dogs, spending almost an hour with each. He is asked not to come on weekends, the busiest days for adoptions, but as a new world begins to open to him he increases his visits from once to twice a week.

The nights are shorter now and turning warmer. Wakeful again, Graves thinks he has heard someone yelling in the street outside, though at first he cannot be sure. Then he hears it again, farther up the street, and someone yells back, still farther away. There is an adolescent waver in their voices, and it is well past midnight. A couple of youths, he concludes, out on the prowl.

He recalls a motel in Denver where he sometimes stayed, an older, two-storied place which had seen better days—the kind of place in which he often found himself accommodated back in his days on the road. Upon his last stop there he was troubled at finding it enclosed by a chain-link fence, topped with barbed wire. Construction, he assumed, but then he began to understand that the former apartment buildings behind it were now a housing project of some sort. The buildings looked worn and prematurely aged, and from his upstairs room he could observe the comings and goings, mostly on foot, of the poor who now resided there. Late that night he was awakened by a gang of youths—both black and white, as well as he could determine—gathered at the fence, hurling their threats and insults. Graves watched warily, thinking himself undetectable in his darkened room, and yet one of the smaller boys seemed to be staring directly and furiously at him. He stooped to pick something up, cocked his arm, and hurled his missile, whatever it was, unmistakably at Graves's window. Involuntarily, Graves ducked, though apparently nothing was actually thrown.

The animal shelter, in a clearing of ponderosa pine among similarly wooded foothills on the far edge of the city, is accessible only by a mile of unpaved washboard road, hook shaped, which ends abruptly by climbing the little knoll where the shelter is secluded. Between the hills are narrow, dry meadows where prairie-dog towns are thriving. When Graves walks far enough in any direction he can see the grand suburban homes which ring the area, and he can hear an unseen bulldozer in the hills beyond, no doubt clearing space for more of them. It seems to him that there are nevertheless countless trails through the nearer hills awaiting his discovery. Some of these, faint and barely traceable, he takes to be pathways worn upon the land by the area's wild inhabitants, and it is in ascending these through brush and around rocky outcroppings that he and his canine companions have come upon the elk and white-tailed deer who must have made them. On three occasions, too, Graves thinks he has seen a coyote—a stealthy, almost spectral presence, keeping its distance but each time watching them, and then reluctantly retreating. Whether or not it is the same coyote, sighted on separate days, Graves has no way of knowing.

At such encounters the dogs will sometimes pull and rear, but more often they stand and gaze, spellbound, like Graves himself. They often begin their walks with such eagerness as to pull him off balance at his end of the leash, but invariably they return at a more docile pace with their tongues dangling.

"That time on the leash is good for them," he is told one morning by Peg, a member of the staff who comes out on her break for a smoke. All of them have grown used to seeing him there, and he is sometimes thanked for his services. "Whatever you're doing, it's working for them."

The reference, he knows, is to the fact that the dogs he walks are frequently adopted. They recognize him when he enters, and, unable to disappoint them, he tends to take the same dogs out again until, arriving of a morning, he finds them missing. He turns to a new one among those he has neglected, regretting, always, the limitations imposed by his fatigue, and then the sequence has a way of repeating itself.

They are treated humanely, as far as he can discern, yet he cannot overcome the feeling on his visits that he is an emissary from the outside world to the imprisoned, a few of whom seem to bear the weight of a death sentence. But even though most have been incarcerated through no fault of their own, Graves is able to read forgiveness and longing in their eyes, eyes which seem, moreover, incapable of dissembling, their emotions being always transparent.

Indeed, as he eases along the rough dirt road toward the graveled parking lot of the shelter, Graves has only to lower his window to comprehend the anguish within its walls, from which the pitched and plaintive vocalizations, the long moans and the drawn-out howls, seem always audible and consummately expressive.

Late in May, on a blustery morning when the wind feels warm, Graves has just emerged from the downtown streets and undertaken the ascent beyond the church, where the sidewalk rises perhaps fifty feet in the course of a block, when he realizes he is not going to make it—not without resting, at any rate. Whereas he ordinarily welcomes the daily ritual of his heart and lungs contending with this modest resistance, his legs are now leaden, and there is a pain near the center of his chest which he has been gradually forced to acknowledge—and which is finally sharp enough to bring him to a halt. Seating himself on a little retaining wall which withholds the sloping yard of a bed-and-breakfast inn, he feels the pain spread through his shoulders and arms, so that even his hands feel dilated and heavy. He hasn't been sleeping well, and a great fatigue consumes him. Resting with elbows on knees and face in his cupped hands, he waits. The pain seems long in subsiding, but when at last it does he stands and slowly straightens himself, then labors with great care until he has surmounted the small hill.

Thinking about the experience during the remainder of the day, he wonders a little that it fails to trouble him, that even at the time it caused him no alarm. If he was not mistaken, he saw the curtains part in an upstairs window of the inn, where a woman watched while he endured his pain. Rising, he glanced up again and saw her vanish with a smile of what seemed recognition. Someone he should have known, perhaps, though he cannot think who.

J. M. FERGUSON, JR.

By midsummer Graves has detected no sign of the band music which distracted him the previous year, though at times, working in his yard, he has stood still to listen. Nor can he recall, without some omissions, the dogs that he has walked and tried to befriend, a circumstance which he regrets, particularly in the case of those who were never spoken for.

He is aware, however, that there is usually a dog who is foremost in his thoughts on the days between his visits, a dog he will be glad to get back to, knowing he will be missed. At present it is a rangey, youthful Doberman mix of cheerful disposition, black and caramel colored, whom someone has named Snickers. Since their first walk together he recognizes Graves at once when he enters, rears up gently against the front of his cage as if making sure he will not go unnoticed, and, ears back and stubby tail wagging, attempts to put his best foot forward. Graves obliges by going straight to him, even though he might subsequently have to pass his cage with another dog in tow. Yet Snickers seems incapable of resentment or any ill will toward man or dog.

Just now, as Graves pauses to catch his breath, Snickers pauses to inquire, turns and rears up tentatively on him, and looks him in the face with his ears laid back and his orange eyes beaming. Graves senses that he is being offered an invitation, an unspoken proposal that they share their lives as companions, and he is intensely aware that the dogs are living beings like himself, his equals, for he has never thought of a dog as a pet, nor of himself as a master.

More than once the possibility of becoming an adopter has crossed his mind, but he has managed to think better of it, preferring to remain the volunteer walker he has become. Then one morning, before he can inquire, he is informed that Snickers has been adopted. He is relieved, as always, but saddened too—he will miss him. He turns his attention to those that remain and those who are new, resigning himself. It is all a part of some cycle, he prefers to think, beyond his own control.

"Some of the nicest people I know are dogs," he confides to Chad one morning, not a little surprised at the conviction in his voice.

Chad gives him a look, then smiles and nods, but whether in true agreement or out of mere politeness Graves cannot ascertain.

Another month has passed, however, when Graves first encounters the dog who will come to be most on his mind. He has just returned a white bull terrier to her cage near the end of the last aisle, his third dog of the morning, when, preparing to leave, he hears a barely audible whine, a small complaint which is almost a sigh, not unlike the way his back screen door has begun to squeak, full of pain and longing.

"Well, hello there," he intones, stooping to peer into the adjacent cage where a great shaggy stray, collared with a piece of chain, lies watching him. His tail slowly thumping, the dog gets unsteadily to his feet as Graves eases into the cage and fastens the leash he carries to the chain. He pets the side of the inmate's shoulder, as is his habit, for reassurance, but he feels the big dog tremble slightly beneath his hand.

Outside, he replaces the chain with a nylon collar and stays the extra hour to walk with "Woolly," as he calls him for want of anything better. Subdued and bedraggled, the dog walks slowly, and twice they must pause for his bouts of coughing and choking. Still he seems grateful, glancing back frequently at Graves as if in disbelief. And so begins for Graves the last great love of his life.

At home, hearing his screen door creak, he is smitten with sudden compassion. He increases his visits to three days a week, going first of all to "Willy," as he alters the name just slightly. His condition seemingly on the mend, Willy has a way of sauntering now as he walks slowly and close to Graves, his spine and hindquarters weaving gracefully, suggesting a cautious optimism.

Though he hazards no guess as to the mixture of his lineage, Graves finds his new friend beautiful, with woolly flopover ears and a heavy but well-shaped muzzle which finds its way disarmingly into his lap whenever he sits to rest. On such occasions he reaches over Willy's back in a kind of hug and pets his shoulder and flank, feels his heated breathing despite his deliberate pace, the metabolism burning faster than his own, then scratches behind and between the ears where the fur is dense but not so long. When he allows his hand to rest, the dog's eyes, glowing warm and amber, roll around and seek his own. He has only to lower his face to feel his cheek caressed by Willy's tongue.

One morning in their third week together Graves pauses without sitting down, having overheard something delicate and arresting, perhaps the carol of a Western tanager, the wonderful bird which he hears now and then throughout the summer but seldom sees. He listens, and he realizes that what he hears is a human voice, pitched high and clear, a woman singing. He follows in pursuit, taking Willy with him over an unfamiliar trail, the intermittent refrains which reach them sweet but seemingly no closer. At length, topping a hill, they look down upon the glint of the morning sun on a bicycle—pushed along by the singing girl who is dressed in shadowless white, her long hair shining. As they watch she disappears in a pool of shade, beyond which the path bends out of sight.

They follow and reach the bend where the girl has vanished, but the singing has long since ceased. The trail forks, they can see, and the one Graves knows they should take is blocked, in part, by a token barricade of stones. He halts again. It is not the stones—there is room to pass around or even between them—but the whitewashed warning he has read on them which gives him pause: "Never...Death...No Hope...Stay Away," he reads again. He is not superstitious, he reminds himself, but he considers Willy, who is looking up at him and patiently waiting. He hesitates, then leads Willy around the stones, and eventually on a trail they at last come upon which he recognizes, back to the pound.

Graves is awakened that night by the barking of a dog at some distance down his block—a small dog, it sounds like, though one which he cannot identify. It is just past one o'clock, and he listens for the voices he suspects he will be hearing in the street, the shouting and the rude laughter, and yet he hears nothing. The barking has stopped, but he goes to the window to look. The street is empty, and the silence seems absolute. Through his parted curtains he can see the thin sliver of the moon overhead, and, not far removed from it, a remarkably bright planet.

Graves returns to his bed but remains sleepless. He suspects that the planet is Jupiter, but he has never known much about the heavens, and so cannot be sure.

On what turns out to be their final walk together, Graves takes Willy to the hill where he has often seen the elk, an area he has avoided since the rutting season, but the season is by now well past, and he knows Willy to be too gentle to make trouble.

The narrow path they use, requiring a gradual ascent, is shaded most of the way for them. They see no elk, but when they have gained the clearing at the crest of the hill he detects some movement near the forest's edge, and there, within perhaps fifty yards of them, he counts six white-tailed deer bounding gracefully away in the mottled light between the trees. He stops, kneels, and tries to point for Willy, who also stops and then stares as one and then a second straggler goes bounding to catch up with the others, all of whom then fade from their view, deeper into the forest. It seems to Graves that he and the dog he kneels beside, in their moment of observing together beneath the late September sun, are in some way a single entity, transfixed and yet transported. When the deer are gone Willy looks at him with eyes reflecting wonder and gratitude, and together they resume their walk, following the dog's slow, sauntering pace.

On their return, at the mouth of a descending draw, they pause in the shade of a mountain cottonwood where, by one route or another, Graves has taken to resting. There, with himself settled on a well-placed rock and his friend's quiet head at rest across his thigh, they can survey the longest of the meadows with its wildflowers—yellow penstemon, purple lupine, Queen Anne's lace—swaying among the sunlit grasses and weeds. At some point, the compassion he has felt for the animal he holds has turned to love, and, momentarily, he rests at peace in the knowledge that his love is requited.

"Good boy," Graves whispers. "Yes, you are a good boy."

J. LEON 01-

At home with the weekend before him, he recalls how each time he returns Willy to his cage the dog, though always obedient, hesitates just long enough to search his face, and Graves can no longer bear it. He doubts that any intervening adoption is imminent in the case of Willy, but by Sunday evening he determines that he will take Willy home with him, and his decision, once made, lifts his heart to an unforeseen lightness.

Yet he drives to the shelter on Monday morning with growing misgiving, until, standing at last before what has been Willy's cage, he confronts the realization of his dread: in the place of his friend are two small newcomers huddled together in troubled sleep, the new card on the cage identifying them simply as "sisters." Graves tours the three remaining aisles to determine that Willy has not been moved, and then, dazed, he begins by taking out another new arrival, willing himself to hope that his missing companion has gone to a good home. Returning and encountering Peg outside on her break, he asks about the dog who has been in W-12.

He watches closely as she recollects, then feels his fear of the worst confirmed in the look she gives him.

Graves hears the syllables "Oh no" escape him, as if from someone else. Unable to speak further, he feels the color draining from his face.

"I'm *sorry*," she offers, then lays a hand on his wrist. "He had the croup, you know, and you were the only one to give him the time of day," she adds, as if to console.

Graves takes out two more dogs that morning, and after that he does not return.

Most of the time one sees perfectly normal men and women passing by the Station House: just now, for instance, a young man with a cheerful and good-natured face, stepping purposefully toward his place of employment. And here is

Graves, entering to claim his stool by the window there, where he deposits his book and his jacket. He goes for his coffee and exchanges a greeting with the counterman—no longer Chad, who has gone farther west to new adventure. He opens his book to read while he sips his coffee, then glances up repeatedly, though he could not say, exactly, what it is he hopes to see.

By afternoon, he is raking the first of the leaves to fall in his yard when the high-school band begins to practice. While the band plays boldly on the nearby field, Graves retreats the good two miles between his home and the public acres known as Buffalo Park, and there traverses the trail which loops another two miles among dry grasses and a scattering of ponderosa before a background of more densely forested mountains. The landscape here, affording appealing but not spectacular perspectives, has always pleased him, but he is surprised to find near the end of the loop that a house has been built where it should not have been. Large and manor-like, it has a pitched slate roof that reminds him of the closed-up church downtown, while from behind scrub oak and pine needles it only partially displays its rather Gothic countenance. Constructed in his absence, Graves reflects, during the six months he has been distracted by the pound, and probably requiring a special access road, unobservable from where he stands, to threaten thus the sanctity of the park—an encroachment which, though vaguely disturbing to him, seems not altogether incongruent.

A little further on the trail, he finds solace in a more familiar landmark. A weathered ponderosa, bare and bereft, dead to the world and yet somehow a living presence, stands in a clearing apart from its fellows. Its towering trunk, an almost perfect spire, is only half exposed to the late afternoon sunlight. Graves sits a while in contemplation, and as the October day deepens, the light on the great ruined tree is imperceptibly displaced by shadow.

When he gets back home it is almost dark, and Graves looks up at the autumnal sky where the first of the soundless planets have begun to glow. The silence is almost eerie, yet not for Graves, whose attention is just then given to something none but he can discern. The band has long since dispersed, and, no, it is not some phantom remnant of it now distracting him, but rather the faintest of disparate barkings, coming not from the neighborhood, he knows, but from further away than a man should be able to detect—from the hills on the far side of the city, if he's not mistaken, from the animal shelter shrouded there in the darkening woods. If he concentrates, as he cannot help doing, there rises in his mind a chaotic din, at the same time barely audible, but gathering itself for an ending in a melancholy howl. He fears they will be with him always, these auditory gleanings—though of this, of course, he cannot be sure.

Lois Taylor

*My cousin Gary has most of his ice-cream cone left. Mine is gone.
He is four years older and we are in Vancouver, British Columbia,
where we were born. Summer, by the look of it. I have only a
handful of photos from childhood—we moved every three years—
and I chose this one because the theme has continued: other people
take longer to eat their ice cream because they think ahead to the
time when there will be none. My cousin looks like a dead-end kid
here, crossed with a Paris street urchin. He almost never bathed,
and played the violin horribly. I thought he hung the moon.*

Lois Taylor was born in Vancouver, British Columbia. She completed her
master's degree in literature at the University of Washington, and has taught,
worked in a city jail as a "personal recognizance" interviewer, served as a
probation counselor, and taken ads over the phone for a newspaper classi-
fied-advertising department. She has published a chapbook of poems,
Learning to Swim, and had poems and stories appear in the *Nation*, the *New
York Quarterly*, *Mid-American Review*, the *Yale Review*, *Northwest Review*, *American Short Fiction*, and others. She also won an Associated Writing Program
award, and a national award for a short story. She has two as yet unpublished
novels seeking publication, *Trouble Breathing*, and *About Time*.

LOIS TAYLOR
Big Moves

I stayed the night on Mother's couch, since she lives close to the airport now. Stony and I talked late on her phone, until Mother came out to inform me, "Some people have to work tomorrow." She felt ambivalent about Stony, everyone did.

Stony was married.

One year, no kids. No matter how fast I say it, it's *married* people hear.

I'd led a quiet life. Sometimes I missed it. Other times it seemed like a dress rehearsal and not a life at all.

I had my apartment and my cat. The landlady had accepted the cat but she'd made it clear when I moved in, "No men roommates. It always ends in violence."

I had my job. I liked to take long walks. I liked the zoo. I'd moved from Palo Alto to live in an actual city, away from the peninsula and its suburbs. This was more real. I wasn't even lonely. I was forever being matched with guys my friends found, and I met a lot in court and just generally around.

I found it easier to be friends with men than being a lover. Love seems to gum the works, and most of my lovers sort of devolved. One way or another, I had a lot of male friends.

And through one of them, I met Stony, who was in town on

a business trip. A group from work, and Stony and two people he was with.

It was the cusp of a three-day weekend and nothing would do but that we all party after dinner.

Stony could both slow dance and swing while everyone else was doing free style. That's where it started for me. Stony is an amateur musician and he liked the pitch of my voice, which in my whole life I'd never given a thought to. You know how it is when someone compliments a quality you didn't know you had? I was Stony's California girl.

Is that enough to break up a home? If I were asked, I'd say no.

I took a cab from the airport into town. Detroit in midsummer. Stony worked at the Renaissance Center. I'd never been beyond Chicago, and Detroit looked bombed out. Empty lots with six-foot weeds. I'd read it was originally dubbed the Paris of the Midwest. Looking out the window I thought, *Bosnia, more like.*

The cab driver had a cousin in San Francisco, which he called 'Frisco. Mother says this hurts her ears, which is funny when you consider that I'm the only family member to ever live in the city.

The driver asked what brought me to Detroit. I smiled and my heart flipped when I said, "Love."

He laughed and shook his head. One thing I've noticed: the respect given love, no matter how gory the details.

He pointed out the Renaissance Center from a few blocks away. Stony hated his job, he hated Detroit. Stony had not told his wife about us. That is, not up until yesterday, when last I asked him.

This meant we'd be sneaking around. I tugged at the straps of my sundress as a wave of panic threatened to pull me under, like a swimmer in strong surf. This is the effect of guilt.

The driver let me out and I gave him a damp and wrinkled

ten-dollar tip I'd been holding the whole ride, on top of the steep fare. That's another thing about love: recklessness. This dress, for instance, I'd charged to a brand new Saks account. I've never had department-store credit cards in my life. The interest is ruinous. That was a word my father used. He died two years ago of a cerebral hemorrhage. He was an accountant, and after he stopped drinking, the kindest man you'd ever hope to know. Stony is a business lawyer, but he was an accountant first. A man on the plane asked me who was this guy I'd fallen for, and I *thought,* He's a married guy, but I *said,* "He's a lawyer, but he was an accountant first," and the stranger said, "Well those accountants, when they take the tie off, watch out!"

Sex talk makes me nervous. It always seems the last thing you need to talk about.

Stony and I drank a lot when we were together and I worried about that, too.

Inside the Renaissance Center I got lost immediately. Stony had said that the building was designed to intimidate. We were to meet at a pub called TGIF.

I wandered until I recognized a woman I'd passed before.

My brother Will, who is also dead, said that when you're lost the best thing is to throw caution to the wind. You're already lost, so go for it.

I leapt onto the nearest escalator and there was the pub, at the top and dead ahead. Thank you, Will.

My brother died of AIDS before people would admit to dying of it. His partner Albert remained a friend of mine, and Albert was withholding judgment on the idea of Stony. "Just don't move to Detroit," he said. "No sudden moves."

"But Albert," I said, "you believe in love."

"You'd both had a lot to drink," he said.

Like my father, Albert was a recovering alcoholic and tended to see through AA lenses.

Sometimes it seemed like there were too many dead people in my life. And drunk ones. My heart beat wildly as I stepped off the escalator. These were the moments you paid the heavy dues for.

He looked so ordinary! I was struck suddenly by the fact that he was mortal and I almost walked away, but then he spotted me and stood, so transfixed that had he been holding anything in his lap, it would have fallen to the floor.

I should explain about Stony's wife. I always do.

Stony met his wife in law school through a study group. Since they were the only reliable members of the group, they were thrown together.

Gradually, she started leaving or forgetting more and more stuff at his house. All very casual. Stony admired her mind. Logical, he said.

Stony was the only one in his group with a house. When he'd turned twenty-one, his parents had given him fifteen thousand dollars, and Stony put part of it toward a down payment—houses were cheap in Detroit—and with the rest he paid his way through law school. My accountant lover.

Stony's wife was a thalidomide baby. Her left arm looked like a claw. She also had trashy-rich parents who left her with housekeepers. Everyone, including Stony, felt sorry for her. Clarice. That's her name. You are not supposed to hurt people like Clarice.

Everyone admired Stony for marrying Clarice. Now, when he hinted to these same friends that he wanted to leave the marriage, they wouldn't even listen. They told him *hush* when he said, "You sleep with her, then." They thought he was saying he couldn't love the arm, but it wasn't the arm; it was the joke. They'd married on a whim, one of their friends officiating via mail-order authority, everyone doing a lot of cocaine, alcohol in abundance, ribs and potato salad. The whole thing—a joke. The subject of love never came up.

Stony and Clarice had simply said, "Hey—let's marry." Tax-wise it was, well, wise.

The trouble was that Stony was joking and Clarice was not, and he knew it. He only pretended he didn't. Because you always know, don't you?

It lasted one year.

Next day was even hotter and I wore the sundress again while Stony played tour guide. I wondered where Clarice was. He'd said she was out of town, but now that I was here, I had to know where exactly she was.

He took me to a Mexican place. We had margaritas and salsa and chips. This seemed funny. He called me his California girl and then we go to a Mexican place. In Detroit.

He was eating very quickly. Blinking, looking around as if bubbles were popping in front of his eyes. We each had two margaritas.

Already my second day in Detroit. I'd seen Belle Isle and the Rouge plant and we'd even driven out to the Irish Hills. I thought these places overnamed, but I kept this to myself.

I loved to touch him. His skin was always warmer than mine. And fragrant. Like sagebrush or my mother's rosemary chicken cooking. He used herbal powders. He was a whole-earth type—no deodorants. I'd learned that staying over last night with him at the hotel.

He'd driven me by his house. He worried about neglecting it, and I knew he meant since last spring, when we met.

I kept my eye peeled for signs of her. I'd never actually seen her in person. I'd looked her up in Martindale-Hubbell, the professional directory. I would describe her as both brainy and sunny. A cheerleader type. Which in fact she was, in high school; somewhere I'd learned that. Actually, Albert knew her slightly, as he knew Stony slightly. Friends of friends. Albert described her as canny, but would not explain.

Stony raised his finger for a third drink now and I went to the "Senoritas" room.

That drowning wave again. Thinking of her, so much more than of myself or Stony or anyone.

I stared in the blotchy mirror and I said, *You are here with your lover and you are going to have a good time! No more sabotage!*

And I went back out and asked him where Clarice was before my behind hit the chair.

He was surprised, and watched as I settled in before he said, "Tampa."

Tampa: the word felt brand new, and silly, like tapioca or tampon.

"Family."

The drinks arrived. I felt nauseated. Much of being in love had these roller-coaster effects. Albert had scoffed: "Think I don't know what it's like, being in love?" Then he went on about all the times he'd been dumped on. "I know, I know, you fix this special dinner and he doesn't show, not even a phone call..." I just stared at him. Albert had gotten it wrong. He was talking about his life.

So Clarice was in Tampa. With family. The wealthy parents. Were they on the water; did she wear a bathing suit? She was such a sport about that arm, everyone had said so.

It was hot in the parking lot as we left the Mexican restaurant. "Detroit summers," Stony had said, "are about moving from one air-conditioned place to another without breaking into a sweat."

The drinks made the pavement waver in front of the car, though that could also have been a heat mirage.

Mirage, I thought. Was all of this a mirage? Which later sounded like the dialogue from a Joan Crawford movie I'd seen on TV not long ago.

But Stony and I did not "get over it"—the unspoken agenda

98   *Glimmer Train Stories*

of my visit to Detroit. I'd gone to see if we couldn't get over it without hurting anyone. This was not going away.

Then for six weeks I commuted between San Francisco and Detroit, and Stony came out when he could. This depleted everything: energy, time, and money. Finally I approached Denise, my boss, about a sabbatical. This was a new concept at the firm, but I had used up all my vacation on those three-day-weekend trips to Detroit.

First, she made a face. This was because we were already understaffed. But amongst the slackers and women looking for husbands, I was at least reliable. I even had seniority.

Then she sighed. "I guess you're good for it."

I moved to Detroit on Halloween. Now we had four more months to see if this would go away.

The flat he'd found was upstairs in an old house—Victorian, like back home. Stony had lived in London and he called it a flat.

He had a futon, a guitar, and a wing chair.

We bought a radio and listened to old shows as the first snow came down. Later we walked through the flakes on ground already frozen and I felt a deep peacefulness I wished I could bottle.

Because a lot of the time, I was drowning. Imagining her. She must be crying, missing him. I knew there'd been scenes. I wondered if he wondered, *Is this worth it?*

I thought of her getting up and going to work. I thought of her in the house, doing his chores. He liked to do his chores. I thought of her arm.

I imagined her clearly, yet I had never seen her in person. She was just so real to me.

This was because he had told me too much. How she'd said, "You love that girl in California, don't you?" That she'd cried so hard he'd had to hold her to keep her from flying to pieces.

He didn't understand that I saw these scenes. They weren't just words to me. It was as if they were happening to me.

Mother had said that if he'd leave one wife he'd leave another.

Albert had said, "Oh, this is definitely bigger than both of you. Definitely." He was being sarcastic, of course.

I came to the conclusion that only strangers believed in love. Your friends were on the other side. Your friends became your parents.

I had a lot of time on my hands and I got to know Detroit better than some of the residents did, or so they said on the bus, at the Art Institute and the zoo. I bussed everywhere and, gradually, I liked Detroit. It was a juicy town.

We went out to hear jazz at places with banquettes and little lamps on each table, like in old movies. We ate barbecue and Coney Islands and bar burgers. We heard Bella Davidovitch play Chopin at Cranbrook and Betty Carter sing at Baker's Keyboard Lounge. We were happy when we weren't sad or panicky.

The time came when my departure was less than a week away, my sabbatical almost over.

We went out at noon to do the laundry, and while our clothes were going around with each other, Stony said, "I know what," and he took us to a bar he used to habituate, near his house.

Stony wanted me to meet Mike, the Irish barkeep. "A real character, a poet of the people," he said.

Mike had a high, sing-song voice, like he was being strangled. He said, "Ah, love, sweet love," as he gave us two pints, then appeared to forget us for some hockey game on the TV. He looked like he was losing a bet on the game.

I felt a little sorry for Stony because I knew how it was when you bragged about people and they wouldn't perform. But we distracted ourselves with darts, and the golden-oldies juke-box.

Stony had been growing slowly angry over the past few days. Not about my departure. About his second-best guitar, his dog, and his carpet.

A divorce was underway and Clarice wanted them, and he would have to give them up, just like he'd surrendered the equity in the house, Michigan not being a community-property state.

He obsessed about them. The guitar, the rug, and his dog.

When I was feeling happy or lucky I'd say, "Hey! We'll buy new carpets and guitars!" though I never mentioned Tricksy. He'd trained Tricksy to wink, and he said Clarice never gave the dog a thought, until the divorce.

"But that's how people get during a divorce," I'd say when I was feeling parental, like our friends. "They get pissy! So what! Grow up!"

"You don't know," he'd say, pulling rank, because I'd never been married. Marriage had been something that might possibly happen, but, like the saint said, just not now.

Mike polished glasses moodily while we sat at the bar, Stony stewing, and I thought I might as well be at home with my family, or what's left of it. This panicked me because our being together was so costly it sure as hell better be worth it.

I watched Stony in the mirror. He was nodding as he thought.

At last he spoke, "The rug is from my grandfather's law office, that's how far back it goes. It's practically family. She's a hippie, basically, my wife. So it's rolled up somewhere and it'll get damp because she won't have the roof fixed either, until one day it'll stink and then she'll go, 'Oh, right: the rug,' and get rid of it, like the goddamn Mafia."

This speech made him so thirsty he raised a finger for

another drink. I got up and played "Crocodile Rock" on the jukebox.

When I came back he was struck by my being there, and he smiled and patted my stool and I sat down.

"I didn't know she was a hippie. Funny. That doesn't fit at all." When he ignored this, I added, "Is it time for the laundry?"

"No. We left forty-three minutes ago. I've got my eye on the clock. I'm on the case."

Stony was a great manager of time. I had always been able to let it go by. I stared out the window and leaves fell, and it passed. For me life was time-lapse photography. I got a big bang out of watching things happen slowly.

Mike brought two more pints, though mine was only half finished. I downed it quickly to hand Mike the glass, as if there were a shortage. The only other person in the place was a steadily drinking guy with earflaps on his hat. I admired this man because, like my father, he had the gift of anonymity. I tended to get noticed. *You look eminently approachable*, my brother used to say.

Stony took a quarter and did a trick with it, turning it over and over between his fingers. He was briefly more cheerful. Then, suddenly, he was not, and his fingers stopped as if they'd forgotten their trick.

What was he thinking?

Trick… Tricksy! He was thinking of that dog again!

He wheeled to me so suddenly my mouth dropped open. He put a hand on my knee. "What say, slim?"

"About what?" I turned to watch us in the bar mirror, where we could be any lovers, not just heartless ones.

"We'll get the laundry first, then—I have an idea."

Outside the snow was mixed with rain, and the skies so heavy it was hard to breathe.

We picked up the laundry, then he drove down the alley

in back of the house. Where his wife lived. With the dog Tricksy.

Some snow was still on the ground, and there were paw prints all over the backyard.

Stony peered over the wheel at the house.

"Ready?"

My heart was pounding; ready was back there somewhere. I was nuclear ready, though muddled. The beer made me thick headed. I couldn't think what I was doing in Detroit, and where I had put my life. Now I was deep in someone else's life. I touched my nose. He saw this and said, "What?"

"Nothing."

"You're sure? I can do this after you're gone. I just thought— with you here—"

I heard it in his voice—Stony had had too much to drink, too; it was either that, or the speed with which it had gone down. Not to mention the hash we'd shared in the parking lot outside the laundromat.

It made me wild, the thought of losing him. Say he goes back to his wife. Say he can't get the transfer out to San Francisco. He dies on the freeway. I'd never seen anything like Detroit driving. I'd thought I'd seen it all, being from California. One Sunday we were driving along in the far-right lane of the freeway to the airport, and the car ahead of us stops dead, middle of the lane. Just stops. A man and a woman in the front seat are having an argument. Then she gets out and runs up the freeway bank. Half-climbing, really, because it's steep. She's dressed as if she's just come from church, including a hat with a veil and bright red pumps.

By this time we've screeched to a stop and Stony has immediately checked the rearview mirror to make sure we aren't about to get creamed.

Then the driver emerges, leaves the car parked on the freeway, and chases the woman up the hill. He tags her, and they continue the dispute right there. Back on the freeway, everyone honks and honks.

Or say he gets sick and dies.

But now, seeing him with that worried look, I said, "I'm fine. Just a little nervous, you know—showing up at her door like this, the two of us."

"Look. Look. She's already got a guy on board."

I turned to Stony. "She does?"

"Sure she does. Didn't I tell you? I thought I told you. Guy we both knew, she knew him first. He was in our class but he didn't pass the bar, something. Took it twice or something. He's kind of a jack-of-all type, or so I hear." Stony peered up at the house again, muttering, "He needs to clean those gutters out."

"Perhaps you can tell him that," I said, but Stony was not receiving.

He got out of the car first. I waited. After a minute he stopped and stared back at me as if to say, *What are you waiting for?* I got out. It was colder for the dampness, just like they always say. Sleeting needles.

Two steps up, a small porch. He rang the bell. I wondered if it was a Detroit custom, back doorbells.

She opened the door. She was very tall. Taller than the two of us. Why had no one mentioned this? We were munchkins. She didn't even glance at me, though she knew I was there. She didn't say a word.

"I'm here for the guitar, the rug, and Tricksy."

I thought: *A man, a plan, a canal. Panama.*

And that very moment, a dog growled.

In the dark hallway beyond her a white dog stood with its ruff on end. Then it began to bark.

Stony flushed so hard his ears turned red. This had to be Tricksy. His own dog barking at him. No wonder he flushed.

"I think you need to see my lawyer. Once you've sobered up, that is," she said.

But she stood aside as Stony, taking my hand, guided me into the hallway where the dog had stopped barking, but was growling.

"Tricks," Stony said to it. The dog looked puzzled.

"The rug's up here." Stony turned from the dog and pulled me up the stairs behind him. I was stumbling and tripping on my muffler, his first gift to me.

A barefoot stranger stood on the landing.

"Hey, man," he said. "You're just making it worse on yourself."

"Top of the morning," said Stony. He dropped my hand.

Then he turned and looked down the stairs. Clarice stood on the bottom step. She was frowning. "The guitar's not up there," she said. "It's in the shop."

"Whatever," said Stony.

He went down the dark hall and opened a door, and there was a draft, then another flight of stairs. We went up them.

It stunk of old paper in the attic.

"I knew it," said Stony, glad to be right. He went to the far end, under steep eaves, and tugged at something.

"Give me a hand?"

"Oh. Right." I went to him and saw a rolled carpet. I lifted an end. It was exceedingly heavy and smelled of cat pee and dog.

We could go only a few steps without stopping, the rug was so heavy. My heart was tripping. The furnace came on with a loud shudder and I cried out. Stony stopped again and turned to me. "Are you all right?" he asked, as if my health were threatened, as if this whole thing was somehow her fault. That's where they were with each other: whose fault is this. I hoped it was a phase.

"I'm fine. Let's just—" I nodded toward the open attic door. I was panting and couldn't talk now. We hadn't let go of the rug.

The man appeared in the entrance, wearing what looked to be women's snow boots now as well as grey sweats. He had long hair, middle parted, like a hippie. He was a little puffy in the face, and very blond.

"Whyn't you just stop now and call it a day?" said the hippie. "You're hurtin' nobody but yourself, man."

We staggered past him, down the clattery stairs, groped our way along the dark second-floor hall, and got to the main stairs.

Clarice was where we'd left her. She looked concerned.

"Samuel," she said. Stony's real name was Samuel, but no one used it; she used it now to be the grownup.

As the caboose, I could not see Stony's face. He did not respond to her.

We started down the stairs, and suddenly I slipped and had to let loose my end of the carpet to avoid falling. The rug slithered from Stony's grip.

"Samuel," Clarice said again.

Now the rug rearranged itself as it pleased all over the stairs, and Clarice had to step down to the hallway, and Stony hold onto the banister. It had come to life, like a Disney teacup.

"Samuel," Clarice said for the third time.

The hippie had joined us, sitting now on the top stair with his chin in his hands, as if we were the floor show. I felt like the hind end of a two-person jackass.

Love has brought you to this. You've come a great distance to be ignored effortlessly by strangers.

"Samuel. What I've been trying to say is, That's not your rug." She leaned forward and they glared at each other, although I could not see Stony's face.

"It's my parents'. From before they moved, remember? They asked me to keep some of the stuff from the Bloomfield house? I don't know where your rug is, but that's not it."

Stony sat down right where he was, half on the rug. He didn't think about tripping and falling. Stony was physically fearless, unlike me. Somehow the rug had buried my feet.

Stony covered his eyes with his palms and sat there.

Clarice looked at him with curiosity. In that moment I saw that she could be cold, and I went weak with relief.

"You can take the dog overnight, and Tom's already put

the guitar in your car. I lied. It wasn't in the shop. But the dog comes back tomorrow, period."

Stony stood and almost fell over. He looked up at me and silently indicated that I should help wrestle the rug back to where we'd found it.

The hippie got to his feet. "Just leave it, man. Enough damage. I'll bring it back up later. Just split, okay?"

Stony ignored him and stared at me, nodded, and picked his way down the stairs over the sullen peaks and valleys of the rug. I followed. Clarice stepped back as we passed.

I looked up and into her eyes as we did. She didn't even bother to focus.

This was a couple with a History with a capital *H*, none of which had anything to do with me. I was dizzy with freedom.

I made it to the car first because Stony was talking to the dog about coming for the night. •

Stony and the dog tore around the backyard growling at each other, the dog leaping, barking. She seemed to remember Stony now.

The dog did several tricks. Sitting up like a tripod on her tail was one of them. The sleet had stopped. Clarice stood in the back door watching with the good arm folded over the other. After a moment, she closed the door and disappeared. She came back with a leash and threw it down the steps for Stony. Then she went inside for good, which you could tell by the slam she gave the door. The hippie watched from the kitchen window. I thought of a woman I worked with, whose kid had seen Martha Stewart on a bunch of her TV shows when he was home sick with the flu. The kid had told his mother, "She sure seems to have a lot of time on her hands."

I drove while Stony talked with the dog and rubbed her ears. They had several routines, which the dog remembered now.

"Where to?" I asked, glancing over. Tricksy had not even bothered to sniff me and she didn't focus, either, when she looked my way.

"We'll stop at a party store for some food for her."

"Can't she eat leftovers?" We grew up with a series of unlucky dogs who ate table scraps and lived in the yard. Mother believed dogs were dirty and my father forgot we even had a dog.

"Leftovers," Stony said, and laughed for the first time all day. "Leftovers! You have to have meals to have leftovers!"

He had a point. Our fridge looked like a bachelor joke. Tonic water and vodka and some withered limes.

We got the food and drove the dog out to Belle Isle, where Stony used to take her on runs.

Stony had a Frisbee in the trunk. I stood watching as they played catch. The dog was really graceful, and I liked the game because nobody won and nobody lost. The dog would not look at me. And when she did, she sniffed and said, *Home-wrecker*, under her breath.

That night the dog's toenails kept me awake, tap-tapping through all of our three rooms and back again. When I got up to brew some coffee, she stared at me until I went back to bed without the coffee.

The light was queer. Like living inside one of those glass snow-scene paperweights, wrapped in weather. Outside the wind blew flakes around, and inside there was a dancing light up near the ceiling.

For the longest time I couldn't remember what that light reminded me of. Just as I was going under I remembered. The light was like the shimmering of pool walls back home.

I packed while Stony watched.

It was decided. He would transfer out west and "we'd see."

His move had already been approved, and all that was between us now was time.

"I don't care," I told him, a lump in my throat, packing and sniffling. "It feels like forever."

"Well, it's not," said Stony.

"Plus, what if you hate it out there and I'm to blame?"

"Hate San Francisco? Long to move back to Detroit? Yeah. Right."

He smiled. I had to smile, too, and blow my nose.

"We'll get a dog," I said, closing the throat of my duffel bag.

He looked philosophical. "Tricksy was Tricksy. It's not a matter of a dog. She didn't even recognize me when I went back."

"I know. I was there."

He shook his head. "It's weird..."

He looked thoughtful for a moment, then added, "Tom's good to her, and that's what counts. He walks her more than I ever did."

I stopped packing as I heard *her*, and understood that now, *her* was Tricksy. Progress.

"You taught her tricks." I checked the drawers one last time. I hate leaving things behind. It always looks like a bid not to be forgotten, and a person needs other ways to be memorable.

"Tricks..." He was lost in memories for a moment.

He brought himself upright. "So. Ready to motivate?"

In our lovesick phase back when I was still commuting, we'd been so busy staring into each other's eyes we'd let my plane lift off without even noticing; it took all day to get home on the local. Now we left early for the airport.

I sat down on the bed next to my bags. I didn't want to go. I liked it here. Not as much as home, that was true; still.

But, as Stony would say, *We've been all over this.*

I cared about him in little and big ways that kept surprising me. And it didn't go away. Not with the thalidomide and the big move and the grabby divorce and the hippie assuming his place. It would take something really big to make it go away.

He stood and lifted my bags and said, "You sure you got all the bricks?" which made me smile, because that's what he always said. Like a real couple.

Pulling away from the curb in the leased Chevy, he said, "We have time. There's something I want to show you."

I wasn't really listening. I was looking up at the house and memorizing our first home for the nights ahead when I would go over it in detail. The blue porch, the Victorian wood lace, the mailbox standing on one leg like a bird. Our curtains. Our window. Our new bed. She'd demanded the futon at the bitter end.

Let her have it, I thought, as we turned the corner. I wish her joy of it.

We went to the river and he got out of the car, walked to the edge, then turned and gestured to me.

I got out and walked toward him. This is what he wanted to show me? The river I'd seen a hundred times?

There was a peaty smell in the air. I began to ask if it was spring I smelled, but he called out as I crossed the stiff grass, "It's the ice. It's breaking. I hoped it would so you'd get to see it. D'you see?"

I did now. A sound like gears changing, like an animal lowing. A thrill went to the center of my being. Like watching from a safe distance as the world is getting born.

The ice was surging past us now in giant chunks. I half-expected to see a polar bear sitting on one.

Ice breaking? My brother would say, *What's a meta for?*

I couldn't stop smiling. Stony was watching the ice.

"See?" he said proudly; "see?" when what he probably meant to say was, *Listen.*

*Siobhan Dowd of International PEN's Writers-in-Prison Committee in
London writes this column regularly, alerting readers to the plight of writers
around the world who deserve our awareness and our writing action.*

Silenced Voice: Burak Bekdil

by Siobhan Dowd

Burak Bekdil

Photo credit: Turkish Daily News

or a peaceful way of life in Turkey,"
wrote journalist Burak Bekdil in a recent
piece for his column in the *Turkish Daily News*,
"you need among your close relatives a doctor, a police chief, a car mechanic, and, most
importantly, a judge ... An ordinary Turk
would probably have a one-in-a-million
chance for a fair trial if he is foolish enough to
trust the Turkish courts and judges... Many people think
Turkey's most untouchable class is its generals. Oh no: never
underestimate its judges."

Bekdil's pithy, dry tone is his hallmark, and for some years he
had adopted it without reprisals from his government. However, the irony of these particular words exasperated those at

Glimmer Train Stories, Issue 42, Spring 2002
© 2002 Siobhan Dowd

whom they were aimed, hitting a raw nerve. Bekdil is now facing charges of "insulting the state and its institutions," and could face up to six years' imprisonment. The charges have been pressed by Minister of Justice Hikmet Sami Turk and the President of the Court of Appeals—Sami Selcuk, the very man to whom Bekdil must appeal if he is convicted.

Aged thirty-five, Burak Bekdil is a seasoned journalist with ten years' experience of delivering news and commentary for the *Turkish Daily News*, Dow Jones Newswires, and Western publications such as the U.S. weekly *Defense News*. He graduated in economics from the Middle East Technical University, and then received sponsorship from the British Council to come to the U.K., where he did a postgraduate course at the University of Surrey. He continued to develop warm relations with Britain on his return to Turkey by becoming Chair of the Turco-British Fellowship Club. In the Club's bulletin, *Keep in Touch*, he describes the Club's mission as strengthening social and cultural relations between the two countries, and proudly mentions that no lesser person than the Turkish President, Süleyman Demirel, is a fellow member.

This small detail reflects the fact that up until now, Bekdil has rarely gone out of his way to chagrin the authorities. Indeed, he is on record as joining his government in its sharp criticism of Abdullah Ocalan, the leader of the Kurdish liberation party, the PKK. In a statement issued on behalf of the Turco-British Fellowship Club, he describes Ocalan as a terrorist with the blood of thirty thousand victims on his hands. His journalistic work can generally be described as mainstream (the *Turkish Daily News* is hardly noted for strident dissent). His stories for *Defense News* are factual and objective, but reveal a close and trusting relationship with top military sources.

However, when he began to write "Equilibrium," his popular column in the *Turkish Daily News*, perhaps he felt it was time to exercise his opinions a little more. One hilarious column from November 1999 describes Prime Minister Bülent Ecevit's relations with the International Monetary Fund as a kind of operatic set piece, reminiscent of Verdi's *Rigoletto*. The Prime Minister does not emerge well. He is described as "once a notorious leftist who condemned 'almost anything American'" who now "wears a shy smile and knocks on the doors of the IMF, which he used to call a 'bloodsucking imperialist organization.'" This is because "he needs money and has learned that money has no ideology."

By March 2001, the tone toughened further. Here Ecevit's defensive rhetoric in refusing to admit to certain economic failures is described as "pathetically tasteless," and Bekdil concludes: "It is unfortunate that the current political picture further sparks growing cynicism and apathy in Turkey. Most Turkish voters tend to believe that nothing ever changes, that all government is equally bad, that all politicians are the same, and that there is just no hope for a genuinely clean Turkey." His use of the word "clean" indicates the general drift of his thinking. Observing corruption throughout the state apparatus of his country, he had perhaps decided that the time had come to use his position as a respected "mainstream" pressman to better effect. By August 27, he was ready to issue his most candid criticism of corruption yet, targeting Turkey's judiciary. His article, quoted above, included a fourteen-point guide on how to survive a journey through Turkey's courts. Little did he realize he might be writing the guide for himself.

In September, he was called to the state prosecutor's office and informed that charges were being pressed against him. He reports that it seems as if "they almost already know what to do about me—even before the trial has started. All this does not look promising." He is asking for international support, not just for himself, but for the cause of freedom of expression in general in Turkey. "I would happily and in the most honored way spend some time behind bars for this article," he quips, but adds that it is more important to draw attention to the circumstances that make such an imprisonment possible.

Please write polite letters appealing for the case against Burak Bekdil to be dropped to:

Prime Minister Bülent Ecevit
Basbakanlik
Cankaya
Ankara
TURKEY
Fax: 011 90 312 417 0476

Amalia Melis

My sister Anna is on the right, shocked by the flash. I'm about as old as my daughter Anna is now (four). I've been pulled to Greece and my sister has stayed on these shores. My husband's created a safe harbor for me, so I am only now prying open the stories locked in my head. "Immigrant Daughter" is the first story I've sent out. I never thought when I played hopscotch with my sister and friends that I'd save our childhood years to write about in one form or another, but family stories and history always had my attention. It all seems relevant and absurd—little snapshots of people just passing through.

Amalia Melis lives in Athens, Greece. She still misses New York when she's in Greece and misses Greece when she's in New York. She's finally realized there is no cure for this condition, so she might as well write about it. She works as a journalist for magazines and newspapers. She worked with Peter Gabriel when he filmed his concert in Athens for "Point of View," and chases down drug traffickers, artists, and anyone else who strikes her fancy for interviews. She also listens, as often as she can, to squeaky violins playing the balo on the island of Andros. She has an MA from the New School for Social Research in New York.

AMALIA MELIS
Immigrant Daughter

Greek Fire: The original Greek Fire was an inflammable sub-
stance invented by the Greeks of the later Byzantine Era,
which they used with a flame thrower to destroy enemy ships.
It was alleged that it could stay alight even under water,
submerged in a contrary environment.

Greek Fire by Oliver Taplin

ournal Amalia Tellos

*We were burnt by a Greek fire. At least those of us who would not
let go. We pushed off Greece's shores even though we were prisoners—prisoners of a place we could not love enough to stay, but could
not let go of. With us we carried heavy parcels that were of little
consequence, but we didn't know then that the biggest burden of all
would be our memory. All of us had chosen, we thought, a temporary
journey away from the world we knew. The earth that had been tilled
by our grandfathers' and great grandfathers' hands would wait for us
because we wouldn't be gone long.*

*We left behind the daily watering of our fields, the chiming of bells
for Sunday mass, the weathered homes whose walls had witnessed the
birth of all our generations. We left, dreaming that this unknown
destination would give us the means to return, to provide for a better
life. Burning like Greek fire in a stormy sea, some of us were able to
stay lit, inflicting the greatest harm on ourselves for surviving. Yet
others went out like shooting stars on a summer night.*

AMALIA MELIS

I chose to leave for America after I lost the flicker in my kandili, *lit every night next to the icons with my prayer, waiting for some word on Petro. Up by the Greek-Albanian borders, Petro was missing in action. A soldier doing his duty for his country, a soldier and a child of nineteen. Leaving behind nothing much, just a patch of earth surrounded by the deadly blue Aegean Sea.*

ENGLISH FOR COMING CITIZENS
By H. H. Goldberger,
Instructor in Methods of Teaching English to Foreigners
Columbia University Board of Education
City of New York, 1946
Publishers: Charles Scribners & Sons
Name of Student: Amalia Tellos
Condition of book when received: Excellent

Foreword

The World War has brought home to us, now as never before, the need for effectively Americanizing the millions of non-English-speaking residents of the United States. The first and perhaps the most important step in this process is the acquisition of English, the tongue in which America thinks and expresses itself: for although the bonds of language are thinner than air, they are more binding than the strongest links of iron.

Lesson One: Colors

Roses are red. The sky is blue. Grass is green. Lemons are yellow. Nuts are brown. Snow is white. Coal is black.

Exercises: What is the color of your eyes? What is the color of a Negro? A Chinaman? A German? An Indian? Name the colors of the following articles which you are now wearing: hat; shoes; coat; tie; collar; shirt. What are the colors of the American flag? Fill in the blank spaces below with the color.

118   *Glimmer Train Stories*

Answers: The ceiling in this room is <u>white</u>. The walls are painted <u>yellow</u>. My hair is <u>black</u>. The cover of my book is <u>brown</u>. Leaves are <u>green</u> in spring and <u>yellow</u> in autumn. An old man has <u>white</u> hair.

The windows were shaking from the wind. The raindrops were persistent. Tonight's English lesson for new immigrants was a bit difficult for Amalia because she was unprepared. Last night she should have reviewed her homework, but she did not.

Journal Amalia Tellos
  My heart is blue. My lemon tree will bloom with the most fragrant white flowers in the spring, but I cannot smell them. Our house stands proud and whitewashed in the sun. My mother is braiding her white hair into a bun. Everyday the same way. Who is helping her now? The grass was green when I fed my goats in the spring. Snow is white. We never had snow in Andros. We had rain. We had winds that would whip up around our house trying to lift the roof off our heads, but no snow. Andros, the Cycladic island of the winds. Coal is black, like the sweater left behind in my trunk. My mourning for Petro will not end. Not even a proper funeral for him; he was never found. Even after the war. Black is a velvet cape covering everything left in my heart. No, not even my daughter or my husband can erase the blackness inside me.

Amalia was the first to enroll for English lessons among the transplanted villagers tucked in the tenement housing at 123 Division Street, lower Manhattan, near Grand Street. Eight families living in a fourth-floor walk-up.

Amalia was proud of herself. She was going to communicate in a new language. She who stood on the deck of the SS *Saturnia* when it approached the Manhattan skyline for Ellis Island, arms wrapped around her daughter, and whispered, "Where are all the white houses?"

AMALIA MELIS

Greek Folk Sayings about Journeys
"Whoever does not have a brain has feet."
"Asking questions will get you into town."
"Nighttime's deeds are laughed at during daytime."

Journal Amalia Tellos

I am on a journey. I am not alone and yet I am totally alone. My body ends at my skin, my thoughts end in my terror. I have journeyed from an outcropping in the Aegean Sea across the ocean to the land of opportunity. What is opportunity? Is it the alarm clock that goes off on Monday and brings me back to the hot shower, the brewing coffee pot, the velvet wallpaper on my wall?

What is a journey? Is it the image I remember before I fall asleep? The small well in Andros that had a slimy green spout but released the most crystal-clear refreshing water God put on this earth? Is it me laughing on my way to the well with my jug? Filling the jug so high that the lemon I used as a plug would pop? Is it the wood-burning stove we lit on winter nights to tell stories by? Or my first visit to Athens from Andros when I looked up on Patision Street and saw the most breathtaking view one could see, the Parthenon?

Everyone takes a journey. Some travel from one end of the globe to the other. Others only move down the road to take on a husband and keep a life no different than the one they have always had. Others travel and can never find a home except in specific moments.

Those tender moments, soft and transparent like soap bubbles floating until the slightest pressure, the softest obstacle makes them pop. Moments that arrive in a lyric, in a line of poetry, in the smell of the earth after the rain. Moments that let me belong.

Springtime in Andros comes like Persephone, shouting her arrival. Goddess Demetra spreads deep red poppies to greet me in the fields. In our village it has been said that the poppies are like drops of blood that have fallen there from the thousands of battles that have taken place on that ancient soil.

120

I remember the baby lamb playing at my feet. I stepped on chamomile and the delicate aroma accompanied me throughout the day. I used to go home hungry from our fields, digging ditches for the watering at night. Around each lemon tree and olive tree, I dug neat strong trenches to catch the town's water that was ours from three to four in the morning.

I own twelve olive trees; my brothers own three times as many. Although it was me they had to provide a dowry for, I am worth only twelve olive trees. When asked, my father says he has three children and one daughter. I am but a daughter.

Lesson Two: Hours of Work

The men in our shop work nine hours a day. We begin work at eight o'clock in the morning. At twelve o'clock the whistle blows. We all stop and go to lunch. At one o'clock the whistle blows again and we begin work again. We work until six o'clock. Then the whistle blows for the third time and we stop for the day. On Saturdays we stop work for the day at twelve o'clock and we go home for lunch.

Questions: What is your business? Where do you work? Who is your employer? How many hours a day do you work? When do you begin work? When do you stop work for the day? How long do you work on Saturdays? Where do you eat lunch?

Amalia sat on the chrome chair by the paper-towel dispenser. Her varicose veins were hurting her tonight, making it difficult for her to stand as she usually did, chasing the women to each sink, paper towel at hand. Of course that meant fewer tips, but she was so tired that she didn't care.

Silver Palace was in full swing tonight. Working in the bathroom of this tattered catering hall in Astoria was all she had left. The rent had to get paid and the grocery coupons needed to transform themselves into dinner.

AMALIA MELIS

The door of the bathroom swung open letting the island music from the dance floor sneak in with the two young women. The sweet melody of the violin and *santouri* made Amalia sigh. On and on the songs went. First a *balo* and then a *sirto* dance giving those gathered there an excuse to get up, join hands, and become part of the throbbing, dancing, semi-circle of girls, mothers, aunts, boys, and men all somehow connected to Andros.

Tonight was the annual Andros Dance held by the descendants of those who left, those who never found a way to return to their homeland. She was one of the ones who stayed behind in this new country, so tonight was especially difficult for Amalia.

The two young women continued to giggle and whisper. "So I says to him, not here, someone might see us. It's too close to home."

"Then what happened?" asked Tzeni, a brunette in a gold lamé jacket, black mini dress, spike heels.

"Well, you'll just die, but Johnny pulls out this little box and puts it practically in front of my nose and says: Will you marry me?

"So I says, Yes, yes, yes!

"It was so romantic I just wanted to die. So then I forgot all about where we had parked his car and I really let him have it. He just moaned and smiled all the way to my house."

"Oh, Mary, you're so lucky. Both of yous. Tom is such a pain. He's just busting my balls by making me wait," whined Tzeni. "Shit, you know, I finished Tammy's Beauty School two months ago, what else is he waiting for?"

"Your turn will come, sweetie," Mary grinned.

Amalia practically had to wedge the paper towels under their arms to get them to notice her. They took the towels but went back to gazing at the diamond chip on Mary's finger.

They turned their back to Amalia and walked out without leaving a tip.

"Stupid girls," Amalia muttered under her breath. She slid back into her chair and closed her eyes.

Lesson Three: Eating Breakfast
  The table is set. A clean tablecloth covers the table. A knife, a fork, a teaspoon are beside the plate. The bread and butter taste good. The wife brings a plate of oatmeal. The man eats the oatmeal with sugar and milk. Then the hungry man drinks a large cup of coffee. Things to eat for breakfast: Fruits: oranges, pears, berries, plums, apples, melons.
  Questions: What do you see on the table? Who is sitting at the table? What food is on the table? With what does the man eat the oatmeal? What does he put into the coffee? What do you eat for breakfast? What would you like to eat?

The feast of Agia Marina in Andros was Amalia's favorite. She woke up early before her mother, fed the goats, gathered the day's eggs, and was back inside before her brothers woke up. Not much was stirring in the village yet. She dipped the dry bread into her glass of warm milk and got dressed for church. Papa Yiannis rang the church bells loud and clear, summoning all of them, young and old, to get ready before the second ringing of the bells announcing that the first service would soon end.

Inside the church the incense hung in the air making it hard to breathe on this hot July day. Beads of sweat were beginning to appear on the upper lips of some of the better-dressed women seated to the left of the altar.

To the right of the altar were all the men. The two older men responsible for collecting the day's donations got ready. One started the procession by passing the basket to collect coins, while the other would spray the crowd with perfumed water. Sometimes the perfumed water fell in the eye and stung for a long time.

Amalia spotted Petro, who was already looking her way. She would get a chance to see him at the feast later that night and it filled her with incredible delight.

Synantysis Taverna was hosting the village's feast celebration. The sun finally hung itself over the horizon with great relief. Everyone, dressed in their Sunday best, was slowly moving into position, choosing the best table with a view of the musicians and the dance floor. Maria had to sit next to Yiorgia, the butcher with the baker, the cobbler with the carpenter. Amalia and her family had a table near the violinist.

The sweet melody of the *balo* began. Amalia saw an arm drop the neatly ironed white handkerchief gracefully into her lap. Amalia turned around in her seat to see Petro standing behind her, waiting for Amalia's father to nod with approval for them to dance. The nod came and into his outstretched hands she gently placed the handkerchief. The *balo*, the Cycladic mating dance, swept Amalia and Petro into a circle that closed them in. Petro took two steps and she responded by dancing two steps around him. Before long all the faces around them blurred.

The bathroom door swung open and Amalia jumped to her feet remembering that she was still at Silver Palace. The night would be over soon.

At 4 A.M., Amalia pushed the Silver Palace glass door open and walked briskly into the frozen air that assaulted her nostrils. She lulled herself to sleep on the slow-moving double-R train that made its way to Ditmars Boulevard.

The abrupt, static voice announcing, "Ditmars Boulevard, last stop. Mike, close this one up until the 6 A.M. run," made her jump. She ran out just in time before the train doors closed. Amalia clutched her collar as she raced to her rent-controlled apartment at Rosemary Court. She wanted to crawl under the covers before the morning sun would find her.

Astoria, the heart of little Greece in the Borough of Queens. Rows and rows of attached townhouses and brown apartment buildings. Part of New York, yet so different from Manhattan. The BMT double-R train line ran straight down 31st Street like a spinal cord neatly sectioning off Beebee Avenue and 36th Avenue in Long Island City. Long Island City was a no-man's land that housed the warehouses and factories from the Greek neighborhoods that started at Broadway, went through 30th Avenue, Hoyt Avenue, and ended in the heart of little Greece, Ditmars Boulevard.

Greek churches, barber shops, delicatessens, and bakeries lined both sides of the wide streets. Sweet vanilla would sneak out from Pyrgos Bakery and beckon Amalia every time she walked by. The white powdered *kourambiedes* piled high in pyramids made her remember the powdered sugar she and her mother would pat on each other's noses when they baked the sugar cookies for Easter, Christmas, and every other holiday.

The Con Edison power-plant tower at the edge of 31st Street burned bright, a torch for even blind men to find their way home by. Shrunken men were returning from the night shift, metal lunch boxes in hand.

Getting home was easy now after all these decades. Now she knew by heart to get off at the last stop of the double-R, BMT line. Take 31st Street straight down to the last block. The Con Edison flame burned morning and night like a *kandili* to guide her home. Amalia smiled when she remembered back to her first weeks in New York City before she moved out to Astoria. Newly arrived from Andros, she tried learning about city streets with their corners, lamplights, and store-front windows.

When she took her first stroll alone she spotted a red dress in the store window and made a mental note of it. It helped her find her way back to the apartment house, which looked like a box sliced in four and held them all in, two families to a floor. But the next week when the store changed displays, it changed her mental map. No red dress, no left turn, no way back home.

Trikoli, her village in Andros, had small winding paths that led to an aunt's or cousin's house and a little further down to the priest's house. No streets with corners, cars, and window displays, just droppings from passing donkeys or goats. Sariza Spring with its famous mineral water was at the entrance of the town. The villagers had to climb 350 stone steps up to Trikoli to get to their homes, and that had to be done before midnight because the few lamps that lit the mountainsides were turned off to save the village on electricity.

Journal Amalia Tellos

I go to work each day. I try to be grateful that I work in Silver Palace. I hear the music from my island; I hear all their music. They come in, from Andros, from Karpathos, from Thessaloniki, all over Greece. All of them just show up here in Silver Palace. They bring their longing, their need to belong, to hear the music from a country they were once a part of, but no more.

I never did go back to the island with my daughter. I sent her. I sent her father. Like searchlights I sent them to find what I was looking for. They came back with stories to fill my afternoons. With jugs of green olive oil, with Uncle Socrates's freshly made wine. They came back to me with empty offerings. Oh, to soothe this ache.

I could call the charter company tomorrow and, like the rest of the Andriots, book a flight for summer rest. I could go back like Santa Claus and buy my way back into their memory with gifts and trinkets from John's Bargain Store, but I will not.

Lesson Sixteen: Becoming a Citizen of the United States

Mr. Nelson was very happy in his new position; still, he felt strange and not entirely at home. His friends and the other workmen in the factory often asked him this question: "Are you a citizen of the United States?" He heard many other people answer this question proudly, "Yes, I am a citizen," but our friend had to answer truthfully: "No, I am not yet a citizen." One day Fred Stone, his neighbor, said: "Tomorrow we shall have little work. Let's go to the courthouse and get our citizenship papers." So the next day both men went to the courthouse. The clerk asked them many questions and told them what to do to become citizens of the United States. He told them that they must live five years in this country before they could get citizenship papers, and that the first step toward getting them is the filing of a paper called a declaration of intention. Two years after filing this paper, they must apply for the certificate of naturalization, or citizenship paper.

They decided (made up their minds) to file their declaration of intention at once. Each one of them answered the questions put to him by the clerk. They signed the paper and swore that what they had said was true; then they paid the clerk one dollar and received from him a copy of their declaration of intention. The clerk told them to keep this paper and to attend a night school so as to learn about our government.

Questions: Where were you born? <u>Andros, Greece.</u> At what place did you board the ship which brought you to this country? <u>Patras, Greece.</u>

GREEK FOR AMERICAN CHILDREN:
Language, History, Literature, Culture
St. Michael Parochial School, New York, 1969
Publishers: Divry, Inc.
Name of student: <u>Amalia Pappas</u>
Condition of Book when Received: <u>Excellent</u>

Section One
1453, Byzantine Empire; 1453–1821, Ottoman Occupation and Frankish Occupation of Greece; 1821–1830, Greek Revolution, War of Independence from Turkey; 1830–Present, Modern Day Greece

Topic One: Joys and Sorrows of Everyday Life

1) Are Greek traditions and customs maintained today? Give examples.

2) Observe the photo showing the interior of a Greek home. Compare it with the interior of a modern home today.

3) During the Ottoman Occupation, the Greek slaves named their children after the ancient Greeks. The Turk Pasha said, "You Greeks have big notions in your head. You don't christen your children Yiannis, Peter, Kostas. Rather you choose names like Leonidas, Themistoklis, Aristotle! Surely you have something up your sleeve." Discuss the Pasha's comments.

Section Two

Greek Alphabet, Pictures with Pronunciation

La La Ola. La La Lola. Lola ela Lola. Na ena nini. Ela nini ela. Ela nini nani.

St. Michael Greek Parochial School in Astoria was the only private school for Greeks to send their children to. Parents considered it a sanctuary; students knew it was corporal punishment. Teachers and books were imported from Greece. Smacks and knuckles bleeding from broken wooden rulers were mixed in with daily doses of memorized prayers for religion class, Greek mythology, Greek grammar, and the Greek alphabet. We were kept away from public schools, away from mingling with *Amerikani*, away from the people who scared our parents.

Even though my sister and I considered ourselves Greek, we didn't want anything to do with the new crop of Greeks who were multiplying in our neighborhood. Tight bell-bottom pants, shirts unbuttoned down to their belly buttons, greasy hair—these people could not possibly think they were like us. Whenever one of them passed us in the street and dared to blow a loud, wet kiss, we would scream back, "Stupid Greenhorn." We ran every time and none of them could catch us.

The latest thing among St. Michael girls was meeting some Greek-American guy whose name I did not know. They signed their name on some documents and got lots of money. Greenhorns like the ones we saw on the street bought the fake marriage licenses and green cards. It sounded stupid to me, paying money for a green card.

My father would kill me if he saw me even looking at a boy.

My friend Irini got money for signing her name and she called me pleading on the telephone.

"You have to help Gerasimo's friend, please, Amalia, just sign the paper for him. He's cute. You won't get caught and you'll get money. The FBI is after him and he'll get sent back to Greece if you don't."

"No way, I'll get killed. Did you do your current-events report for Monday?"

"Oh, Amalia, all you think about is school and your stupid poetry books. You are such a pain. I'll see you on the bus. Bye."

On Sunday the Paralikas Greek radio program was suddenly interrupted. An announcer talked about guerillas fighting a war in some jungle. Then he listed numbers killed and numbers wounded.

"Why are gorillas fighting in the jungle? Are they fighting monkeys?"

My mother reprimanded me in Greek. "Amalia, set the table. Baba is hungry and the food is getting cold!"

There were no jungles in Astoria, and the only wars I knew about were the ones in my house, in my neighborhood, and in my head. The My Lai Massacre and Lieutenant Calley were also mentioned in the same news report on the radio. I tried to memorize the name of the Vietnamese village for the current events test by remembering the words for "he talks" in Greek—*milae*.

The Sunday *Greek Tribune* newspaper wrote about a major drug bust at the Megas Alexandros Bakery on Ditmars Boulevard and 33rd Street. On the ground floor were all the *kourambiedes*, chocolate cakes, *baklava*, and pastries we looked at every Sunday on our way to church. Upstairs from the bakery, though, I heard my father whisper to my mother, was a gambling room and women for hire. The Greek mafia was moving drugs through there. The worst part was when I heard him say four people were arrested in connection with fake green cards. The Megas Alexandros Bakery closed down following the police raid. No more cookies after church.

Megas Alexandros, or Alexander the Great to my American friends, was a great Greek warrior, a conqueror of many lands. But now his name belonged to a bakery whose owners had been arrested and shamed the rest of us because they were also Greek.

It rained on Monday, February 8. My navy blue socks were still damp from the rain that missed my umbrella at the bus stop. Shivering, I slid into my seat. Over the intercom Mr. Baziotis's voice announced morning prayer in Greek. Time to stand up.

"*Agios o theos…*," I did my cross three times. The thumb, index, and middle fingers joined together were brought to my forehead, then down to my belly button, over to the right shoulder, and then to the left.

Right after prayer my name was called over the intercom. I straightened my uniform skirt as I skipped two steps at a time down the stairs to the principal's office. Outside, my grandparents stood by the glass doors at the entrance. They were going to the supermarket with the shopping cart. My grandmother gave me a package to give to my mother. She turned

to my grandfather and said she didn't feel very well, she was going home. After my grandfather took off alone for the supermarket, she turned and kissed me goodbye. She grabbed my arm, pulled me close to her, and whispered again:
    "Goodbye Amalia, *s'agapo*."
    "I love you too, Grandma."

    I was the last one to see her alive. She went on a journey. A deep, deep sleep overtook her after she swallowed all her pills. Her limp body left its last breath in the emergency-room hallway of Trinity General Hospital.
    She wanted to get better.
    She wanted to forget.
    She wasn't well.
    She was crazy.
    She was moody from when she was young.
    She didn't know what was wrong with her.
    She said she should have never gotten married because she knew she was sick.

Journal Amalia Pappas
    I was born a daughter. According to tradition on our island, if the baby is a girl the mother gets to pick the name. Even though I was born in Manhattan, the long arm of tradition made its way to Misericordia Hospital and urged my mother to choose her mother's name for me—Amalia. My name was changed to Amelia in the translation, as Amalia was impossible to pronounce in English. But even Amelia was sometimes mispronounced as Amanda. I hated the name Amalia because it wasn't American and smooth sounding like Jessica or Heather. Most of all, my younger sister couldn't pronounce it either, which convinced me I had surely been adopted.
    When those gold name necklaces became popular in grade

school I made sure my mother got me one with the name Emily engraved on it. If I wouldn't be Amelia, and couldn't be Amalia, then I would be Emily, which was Emilia to my Greek relatives and sounded close enough to Amalia. Eventually it became Em for short.

So today I am Em to my sister and two childhood friends. To my American neighbors I am Amelia. In Andros I am Amalia, spitting image of my grandmother with her high forehead. I have come back to her.

I have kept the package she gave me that day in grade school. In it I found her book, *English for Coming Citizens*, with her answers penciled in, and some poems written by the Greek poets Yiannis Ritsos and Nikos Kavadias.

Submission

She opened the window, the wind struck,
with a burst, her hair, like two big birds,
over her shoulders. She shut the window.
The two birds were on the table
looking at her. She lowered her head
between them and cried quietly.

by Yiannis Ritsos, translated by Nikos Stangos

A Bord del' "Aspasia"

Hunted by fate, you travelled towards
Switzerland, the pure white but grieving;
always on deck, in a chaise longue, skin yellow
for that dreadful but all too well-known reason.
Your people uneasily fussed around you;
indifferent you gazed out to sea. All they said
raised only a bitter laugh, for you knew
your journey would lead to the land of the dead.
One evening, as we were passing Stromboli,
you turned to someone, laughing, to speak:

AMALIA MELIS

"How my sick body, here, as it burns,
is like that volcano's flaming peak!"
Later I saw you in Marseilles,
lost, without looking back, as you left.
And I, who loved only the watery waste—
you were someone I could have loved.
by Nikos Kavadias, translated by Simon Darragh

Journal Amalia Tellos

What do we do? The immigrants who have washed ashore here with our dreams, our illusions, our pathetic anticipation of finding the streets paved with gold. We pretend. We, the "xeni," pretend we are close to packing up and leaving. A few more years and we'll be out of here. Same old song, same old wish. The children are still small; we could move back and they will be able to adjust. They will learn Greek; they will be better off there.

Washing dishes at the diner will get us just a few more dollars and then we will be set. Or all those Greek hot-dog vendors spread out all over the sidewalks of Manhattan and Queens who keep saving and saving for the three-story house they will build when they get back to Greece. They just stand there in the rain asking, Mustard or sauer-kraut?

Each one of them dreams, adding up the apartments they'll get to keep when the builder is done—one for the wife and himself, one for his Marika, and one for his Soula, when the girls need their dowry.

My circle is closing. I have gone to confession like the good Ortho-dox Christian I have been taught to be. I married a quiet man—his silence all these years has fed my terror. I became a mother. Although the umbilical cord attached my daughter to me, I have been unable to give her wings to escape the curse of being a daughter. She is defined as her father's daughter. I am defined as my father's daughter. My granddaughter is defined by her father's name.

Time has moved on in my village and it cannot take me. I am here with no roots, no history to guide me. I will not be the

134   *Glimmer Train Stories*

lighthouse for my granddaughter after all. I am a small fishing boat that is leaving.

I am leaving. I am leaving. The blue Aegean Sea swirls around me.

Robert Chibka

From the first time she climbed into his crib to pacify him by reading the funnies aloud, explaining "he was afraid of rabies because he could hear their footprints," Joan was known for playing nicely with her little brother. Here I'm giving my gigantic sister a lift in my 24-Hr. Towing Service truck on the roof of our tiny apartment building in Portland, Maine—an excellent play area we called, with unaccustomed grandeur, "the piazza." While she smiles obligingly for the camera, my expression bespeaks a no-nonsense attitude toward vehicle repair as fodder for narrative invention. I am a man with a mission: barely visible, extreme left of frame, the shadow of the handlebar of a disabled tricycle, our emergency roofcall, which the paparazzi (or mamarazzi) rudely interrupted.

Robert Chibka's first car, a nameless 1973 Dodge Dart, died in late middle age of ferroporosis as a result of elemental exposure. His first novel, a 1990 Norton called *A Slight Lapse*, succumbed, much younger, to *under*exposure and thickening of the prose. Chibka, whose "Thrift" appeared in *Glimmer Train* 31, lives in Boston.

ROBERT CHIBKA
Muffler

I scorn your ideas in order to consider them in
all clarity and almost as the futile ornament of
my own; and I see them as we see in perfectly
clear water, in a glass vase, three or four goldfish
swimming around, always making the same,
always naïve, discoveries.

—Paul Valéry, *Monsieur Teste*

s usual, as always, as ever, the coffee station
functions only as an eyesore. The maker itself—glass carafe
striated cloudy, stainless reservoir stained by axle grease—is
the least disturbing element of the spectacle. Dried spatters
give tan testimony of former functioning: the machine has, in
living memory, been dripworthy. One foam cup, orphaned
from the nesting stack, lies like a beached grampus, highlight-
ing, by unnatural brilliance, ambient untidiness. Conversely, a
pair of sugar packets landed in a coffee puddle, since evapo-
rated; their wrinkled beige desiccation makes luckier packets'
bridal hue look fragile, false. Grey pawprints on creamy label,
lid askew, a jar of noncreamer tall enough to look proud of
itself has strewn powder about, as if to seed sodden Formica.
Balsa-wood swizzle-splints splay at thoughtless, pick-up-
sticks angles.

Glimmer Train Stories, Issue 42, Spring 2002
©*2002 Robert Chibka*

Like something's aftermath, is all Baxter can think. Scene of the crime.

Caffeine, anyway, might not hit the spot; worse, could hit some metabolically proximate, unpredictably side-effectual spot. His out-of-season prescription has Baxter feeling oddly... *muffled* would play neatly on words without inaccuracy, but *hollow* seems more apt. As if centrifuged till liquid innards fled to peripheries, then quick-dried, light and brittle as a wasp nest (but all the same, yes, muffled, as if in gauzy layers). Dry winter air amplifies effects of the pill that, till today, he's used only for late-summer allergies. Well, a side-effectless wonder drug would be asking a lot, wouldn't it. Compared to prior years' over-the-counter counterpollen strategy—antihistamine wiping him out, decongestant wiring him up, interacting in a shifty moiré of zip and crash, yoyo too tame an image, more like carnival rides whipping about in two or three planes at once—compared to that Tilt-A-Whirly sensation, this intimation of innerlessness, of concavitation, is nothing. An unpleasant nothing, to be sure, but nothing nonetheless. And compared to the office—fumes and particulates his pill failed to fend off, of paint, carpet, sheetrock, tile, and caulk, that by midday transcended hay-feverish annoyance to imperil, it seemed, respiration, and make him flee despite substantial paperwork backlog, thanks to weeklong renovational shutdown on top of Thanksgiving not so long ago—compared to that, this maculate but non-toxic venue might seem nearly cozy, if he could ignore loud TV and louder signage and keep his eyes from homing on that sorry coffee station and the felt-tip scribble taped up behind it: PLEASE HELP YOURSLEF.

(Same dumb misspelling annoyed him a decade ago in the single-A Elmira locker room: HEY PIONEERS—CLEAN UP AFTER YOURSLEF! Stayed that way all season while Baxter declined from everyday starter to situation player, till the night Barlow called him in after a tough loss: parent club wouldn't re-sign him, but hey, he's lucky one, B.A. fall back on, do somethin' life 'sides play ball, sad case bein' phenoms signed straight outta secondary, barely read nor write. Baxter didn't bother to correct him—B.S., not B.A.—but that night fixed the sign, two U-turn arrows indicating the letters should be transposed. Next night guys knew who'd done it, ribbed him and rode him, *Puffessah Baxtah*ed him half to death till Barlow said knock it off and suit up, in a tone that let the whole squad in on his secret, then started him in center, first time since July. Made a shoestring catch the home crowd loved, went 0-for-three with a sac fly, then set a record—longest, hottest shower in franchise history—and cleaned out his locker, but not up after himslef.)

More irksome than the honest grime of coffee station or so-called restroom, Baxter finds the cleanly good cheer of surrounding trumped-up theme-park jollity. Posters illustrating illegal and/or life-threatening asymmetries and miscalibrations project an upbeat fast-food ethos, brightly pitching brakes, shocks, struts, instead of burgers, shakes, fries. Bar graphs and pie charts depict stopping distances, emissions levels, like occasions for celebration. A towhead beams in a posture of restraint, so pleased you'd think he was strapped into a roller coaster, not a carseat available, at cost, as a public service of this concerned franchise and your local Kiwanis Club. Trademark traffic-sign-yellow-and-black scarf (oh, Baxter gets it, *muffler*) 'round his skinny cardboard neck. On the sill behind this 2-D kid: a foot-high pink plastic Xmas tree festooned with charm-bracelet mufflers, striped by certain slants of venetian-blinded light. Imaginary toady in front of an imaginary garden.

Like a crime scene, did he think? Indeed. Headquarters must have been loco to light on so revealing a name. "Every underchassis we touch turns to gold." Damn straight, thinks

Baxter, and (whatever the phrase might mean) fuckin' A.

Infamously seductive lifetime warranty notwithstanding, everyone by now knows how it works. Gettin' kinda noisy underneath, you report in regular-Joe dialect; they cut you off before you can say *muffler*. Have a seat, they'll take a gander. You thumb hypergendered periodicals (*Field & Stream, Woman's Day, Road & Track, Family Circle*), yield to the wall-mounted TV's obtrusive volume, or just stare balefully at that feckless coffee station, looking up from time to time like a nervous *Let's Make a Deal* contestant to guess which bay will clear out next. Finally, some Bubba with Buddy, Butch, or Buster embroidered over his nipple plumps coveralled gluteals on your upholstery, guns it, screeches into a bay, hoists your Mitsubishi on his hydraulic, shines a lightbulb with a lacrosse helmet on it all up under your auto's private parts. He pokes and he prods, then invites you into his sulphurous den to hear the bad news.

Pipes. Always and ever, perennially, pipes. It's your exhaust pipe. It's your tail pipe, your wheezer pipe, your pretzel pipe. He'll clench it with a dino-jaw wrench to show how irredeemably rotten, how very near death's door, one pathetic length of galvanized steel can be. Those moments of pronouncing judgment must be the most satisfying of Butch's workday. And by the way, minor leak, rear shocks? Take care that same time, you want. Plus, some special going on balance, ball joints, slave cylinders, bleeder valves; on absolutely anything but pipes. All the while, you can't peel your pupils off the like-new muffler beaming over you like a benched justice, a throned monarch, just that unbearably smug in its lifetime appointment.

Baxter, at the take-a-seat-have-a-look stage, sees dominos fall, and the prospect of coughing up three figures for out-of-warranty tubing stipples his temperament. At the same time, personal chagrin at failing to flush road salt from underbody more assiduously hones uncharity toward those who any minute now will diagnose and replace extensive pipery plus no doubt attendant hangers and clamps.

Baxter still thinks of the middle-aged Mitsubishi, idiotically, as his new car. These days, the motorcyclical din of its idle suggests not only public shame and failed inspection, but lethal seepage. Under carpeting, who knows what shape one's chassis is in? This time of year, when car windows seem shut as permanently as those of the airtight office whose toxins he fled, he'd be a fool not to consider monoxide wafting imperceptibly through floorboards as rotten, for all he knows, as his pipes.

(Lost his first car to degenerative pipe disease in Elmira. Madness to relinquish an auto for want of a pipe or two—given an exhaust system, the Plymouth would have been almost roadworthy—but the estimate to pass inspection was out of his league. Buster delivered the news with the aplomb of one who sees cars come and go every day of his life. Desperate, Baxter imagined barter: pro-jock endorsement, even-steven for a set of pipes? But he'd been riding the pine for weeks, a late-innings defensive sub or pinch [in a *real* pinch] hitter; that endorsement—"I, who haven't hit one out of the infield lately, take my car to E-Z Muff"—might not be worth much to Bubba's boss, Ol' Man E-Z. For a time, Baxter imposed on his girlfriend Jackie or hitched rides with a middle reliever who'd later make it to triple-A but not the parent club. In August he rented a so-called garden apartment near the park and walked to work past ragweed forests—fully symptomatic because pills could throw off what was left of his timing at the plate—till Barlow gave him the ax. When he did, Baxter's keenest regret attached oddly to the Plymouth.)

You could, he supposes, with people too, see it as all pipes: crusty clogged and constricted arterial pipes; windpipes' bronchio-pulmonary ramifications; whole GI tract one madly devious culvert; pores and follicles venting integument; capillary, neural, lymphatic sluices and byways surreptitiously crisscrossing the bodyscape … Ah, pipes, he thinks, ah, humanity! What organ, then, corresponds to muffler, with its infuriating lifetime warranty? Best guess: brain. Except that you can end up with Irish lace for brains, as his father's father heartbreakingly did, and it never gets replaced, let alone gratis. Then again, the accuracy of his mind-as-muffler conceit is a matter of no consequence to anyone, including, it pains Baxter to think, himself.

Do they think only sportsmen and homemakers, proletarians pining for the Eisenhower years, drive automobiles? Couldn't they seed stacks of *Rod & Reel* and *Redbook* with one *New Yorker*, a single *Harper's* or *Atlantic*? Christ, he'd take a *Public Affairs Quarterly*, a *Journal of English and Germanic Philology*. Look, right there in the near bay, bits and jigsaw pieces of its fiendish piping puzzle strewn on dark concrete: a late-model Mercedes. Is the owner of *that* likely to pick up *Maiming & Mayhem Monthly, Housewives' & Helpmeets' Gazette* ?

Consider: Jaguars, too, must be muffled; Mazerattis, piped. Why, then, do clientele always look like Pintoids, Gremlinistas, broke TransAmmers, and rusty-4x4 folk, people who'd read this stuff, abide that TV spewing, from its untouchable perch near the ceiling, unspeakable family dysfunction and glaring pewter-tone reflections? Porsche and Rolls owners, he guesses, drop cars off first thing, have spouses Saab or Volvo them to work in lieu of hanging around to watch guys pinch their pipes with promiscuous monkey wrenches.

Among waiting customers, Baxter sees no one likely to drive such a vehicle. To his left, a fortyish woman, cocoa-brown, kerchiefed, looks intelligent gazing at air, eyes taut as if intent on a soluble problem. To his right, a receding carnation-pink woman in lemon-lime sweats matching oily blond hair blinks as if blinded by floodlights and scurries through a glossy, too rapidly to get even full-page ads' gists: reading as neuromuscular tic. Near her, an older ash-grey woman, earnest and hushed as if a grandchild and not a machine needed repair. All sitting on their coats where thousands have sat before, shifting behinds edgily, keeping thoughts to selves, looking as weary, as wary, as positively... here's the spot for that modifier: *muffled* as Baxter feels.

Then there's Sandy, a Service Manager if her shirt's to be believed, though she can't be halfway through her twenties. She answers frequent phone calls, most often simply stating business hours, thanking people for calling, with the same polished service-sector wholesomeness she used in logging Baxter's complaint. Now and then, one of the Bu-boys elbows the thick glass door open, admitting a gust of country western to squelch the TV, hands her a clipboard, grabs another. All male on the far side of that door, all female on this (save Baxter). Anything about auto underbellies dictate this? Sandy herself exudes a country-western air: sturdy build, frosted perm and eye-do calculated to eliminate any ambiguity the uniform may incite, pleasant low-pitched no-nonsense banter with axle-greasy mechanics. Not androgynous, but kind of a tough chick, equal emphasis on adjective and noun. Baxter suspects she'd love to lay that manicure on a torque wrench, but unwritten rules of the trade relegate her to the customer-service side of the glass door. Her blouse dubs her guys' superior, but he'd guess she makes maybe half their pay, takes more co-worker flak than the long-suffering skirt-and-stockinged crew in Baxter's office.

You'd think a place that makes a living peddling shocks and springs might install something more yielding than these orange plastic seats molded to cradle in comfort lumbar regions shaped differently than one's own and bolted to metal rails bolted in turn to the wall. Autos on lifts are offset, from where Baxter uncomfortably sits, like fanned cards: beyond

the Mercedes, only two model-indeterminate rear ends, ge-
neric faceted taillight plastic. It's 1991, and designers the
world over not too long ago conspired to tilt noses down as if
for sniffing asphalt, hunch asses up like cats in heat. Used to
be easier to tell by its shape what you were seeing, didn't it?
So many look-alikes, but each, it seems, with its own
exhaustiosyncrasies. All around the bays, gun-metal shelving
displays more zanier-shaped pipes, floor-to-ceiling, than
you'd suppose so uncomical a business could make use of. To
see all this, you have to focus hard, peering through a curtain
of hanging fanbelts; enough to belt a city's worth of fans,
you'd think, though this is one of many franchises.

Out in the lot, poor salt-eaten Mitsubishi meekly awaits its
turn on the humiliating lift.

It's this passive sitting and waiting Baxter hates; once he
gets the verdict, he'll take a walk, find lunch, feel better, at
least a bit freer, whatever the cost. But this benched sense! He
always favored defensive half-innings: out there on the diamond, playing, though what was the outfield, after all, if not a
waiting game ... but must these everyday insights, this under-
tow of stale observation, continue? Keen internal ruts—even
this very sense of unfreedom—so typical, interchangeable: so
screechingly banal.

Speaking of which, a familiar K-Mart-Burger-King-Foot-
Locker-Book-A-Buck apprehension washes once again, splitting its usual difference twixt cozy and creepy, over Baxter: he
could be anywhere in the chain-riddled country, anywhere at
all.

TV, bracketed up near coffee-color stains blooming dahlia-
like at acoustic ceiling tiles' interstices, won't shut its big fat
mouth; stories trying so hard to be incredible that they succeed. Men who unwittingly murdered fathers, slept with
mothers, put own eyes out. Women who (withstanding—and
notwithstanding—camped-out suitors) stayed true for de-

cades to MIA mates confront men who cross-dressed and hid in tents to dodge military service in the same war. Wives whose response to brutish husbands' having raped their sisters and cut out their tongues was to fricassee the kids and dish 'em up piping hot to aforesaid brutes. Princes whose uncles murdered their dads, married their moms, challenged onstage by courtiers whose busybody dads got stabbed by sisters' princely boyfriends (said sisters subsequently losing marbles, floating down rivers), and man, are they pissed. Fathers who, dividing domains, greased squeaky-wheel daughters, subsequently suffering elder abuse. Who makes this stuff up, anyway? Guests squeeze such indigestible stories between commercial breaks; studio-audience insights range from "You stink, man," to "I think you like utterly reek." *Talk* show? Shout show, curse show, more like it.

Baxter thinks the better of suggesting to Sandy, who must have a remote, a switch to C-Span or CNN, but mightn't she reduce the volume a tad? Woman to his left, she of the intelligent air-staring features, takes a second to absorb his request, then trains on Baxter an attitude conditioned by just this sort of programming: "Mister Big got issues with Montel? Montel used to be *semper fi*. Whip *your* ass like heavy cream, that's without trying." She does that snaky neck thing of which Baxter believed only teens capable. Lemon-lime lady, blinking disapproval at the both of them, pages through her periodical yet more rapidly.

Sandy's saved from taking sides by a skinny Butch-Buster named Bob—Baxter's age maybe, looks sixty in an elephant-hide face—who emerges to address the ashily grandmaternal woman Baxter had pegged GM all the way: "Mercedes? All set." He brings it around while she confronts the bill: three hundred and change for a high-end Europipe or two. Does no lifelong warranty apply? the flummoxed elder wonders. Her late spouse always saw to such things. Sandy explains:

Bob indicates right here, see, muffler *per se* was mint; now—smile timed to coincide with successful Mastercard authorization—so are the pipes.

We—the species—have trodden on moons, transplanted vitals, stored gigabytes on pinheads, and a host of other, equally predictable examples. Can't we fabricate pipes, whines Baxter inwardly, from rust-proof stuff? How about what they make those mufflers out of?

But here thunders his Mirage into the near bay, positioned over the Mercedes-warmed lift, implacable piston rising out of floor to hoist it like a plate of prime rib on a waiter's arm in close quarters. And Bob, obligatory Salem welded to lower lip, getting under, peering up, angling his shoplight into cranny and crevice like your all-time crabbiest teacher combing sentences for something to get on your case about. Dead ash drops past coveralls collar to ribbed undershirt; flicking absently at his chin, he backs off for the big picture, scrutinizing Baxter's pipes the way a hustler would a pool table.

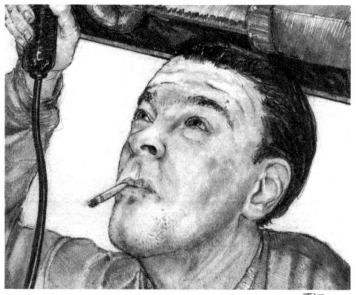

(Just the look Jackie would inflict when Baxter emerged from his makeshift basement study after a day of exhaustive citation, making common cause with this and taking exception to that prior folklorist's assertion concerning morphologies that arguably [or, arguably, don't] transcend place and time, culture and belief, to attain transglobal interpretive robustness. A native Elmiran who'd started seeing a ballplayer with a purple Plymouth Duster and found herself a year and a half later just married to nothing of the sort and already showing, Jackie studied his mug for clues about transcending *this* place [Buffalo], *this* time [snow-drifted outset of his second semester as an M.A. candidate, her second trimester as a ma-to-be]. It was a late dinner—he'd been on the spoor of a thought that might never return—and a bitter-seasoned one. The idea had been for Jackie to work till May, get him through his first year in good standing; after the birth, he'd take a leave, work a semester, a year, till she could support him into tenurable employability. Now, though that look and not *she* said so: Jackie was frosted. He never should have matriculated for spring; a good man would have found honest work the minute he learned she was expecting, even before getting legal, which she'd begun to suspect he'd done dutifully, a shotgun wedding without the paternal firearm. Baxter himself suspected no less, but would never say so; hard to remember *she*'d not said it as she put room-temp dogs 'n' beans before him. Seeking signifiers of amelioration, of any mutability, not she but her look made him cringe, poring over him as a sailor might a cloud bank, a mountaineer a rock face, a grad student a passage. As Bob does an undercarriage…)

Damn this man, this Bob, not only for what goes without saying—destroying Baxter's exhaust system's self-esteem—but for eerily recalling Jackie and their happily long-past sad little married life. She might have made the perfect ballplayer's wife—pretty, compliant, self-sufficient, patient—though he, long since no ballplayer, now finds such traits as off-putting as appealing. And now he can see, it's not just Bob's searching gaze, but icy streaks in Sandy's sandy hair, her chin's quizzical tilt. And it must be, too, Montel with his there-but-for-a-modicum-of-sanity-go-we guests and their each-worse-than-the-last sob stories. This muffler joint calculated, it seems, to send him back to dead Duster, failed career, ill-conceived marriage, the look that made him dematriculate to win bread but that she insisted only meant she'd like more time together—maybe no ideal ballplayer's wife after all—and the miscarriage such a short time later; despite knowing *that*, at least, wasn't literally his fault or failure, how could he not irrationally feel his footnoting zeal had somehow brought it on, put poor Jackie through it?

He's weirdly tempted to abandon his Mitsubishi, just leave it up there with underbelly exposed and flee before this pipemarish scene prompts him to revisit every life trauma, the whole eight years since Jackie gave stillbirth to a lump of regret and the unutterably lucid recognition that the sole sensible basis of their union had now been expelled through the birth canal. Tempted to cut and run, till it dawns on and suffuses him like a drop of dye blooming in water: there *were* no more, that was his final Montel-worthy episode. Since then—he means since the divorce finalized their half-headed, wrong-hearted, misadriot, and malbegotten attempt to do the so-called right thing—it's been, if not a walk in the park, a life of gratifying uneventfulness. Barlow was right: his B.S. suited him for weekday employment, which he tends to use the way Ms. Lemon-Lime does magazines. Like any life, it has its landmarks and round numbers, but it's filled chiefly with pensive untelegenic efforts to avoid falling into, punctuated with repeated fallings into, banality: reaching an age you once thought old; seeing you're not so unlike anyone else; falling out with some, losing touch with others, wishing for more satisfactory companionship. Periodic need for pipes is only the most immediate, fingerable instance of a stable pattern. Irritatingly inevitable, distastefully inconsequential, such moments are neither disabling nor fatal. If banality is the pothole of middle age, Baxter, approaching well below the speed limit, has decent shocks; like that good boy in the Kiwanis carseat, is mostly glad to be belted.

Bob shoulders open the door: "Who's the Mitsubishi?" Squeezing crabwise through the narrow aperture, Baxter is tossing a forlorn look at the cardboard kid just at the moment when—because what else is life but a sequence, at times a simultaneity, of coincidings and incommensuratenesses?—a flash comes from the wall: "We interrupt this program…"; then the glass door shuts itself with a heavy sigh, and the unpre-empted baying of an aggressively cheerful country-western lament consumes them.

Now what? he has time to think before Bob turns to relay his personal bulletin.

Suffice it that the news is not good, is horrid, and if not unexpected (for when and where, to grownups, can bad news be unexpected?), still and all disturbing: a suspension bridge or jumbo-jet down; a standoff, feds vs. crazies; a nursing home's worth of invalids in ankle-high drifts, their facility sizzling behind them; a schoolbus's worth of youngsters reduced to shards for the sins of their (and the bomber's) parents; a city's worth of tap water tainted, the warning too late; a remote region wrung out like a dish towel by plate tectonics; a president, prime minister, or practitioner shot to sudden death; first volley in a war that won't end; comet careening our way—you know all the bulletins, take your pick.

Bob has good hands, big enough for sports: staunch, fearless fingers, filthy, shapely nails. He runs all ten through blue-black grease-slick hair, straight back, temples to nape, then circles thumbs over tips like someone inviting a bribe. It's just his way of preparing to speak, like guys in the office who tap pens or hitch up trousers.

This is worse, Baxter thinks, than I thought. He mustn't forget, something no doubt infinitely worse is this minute being announced next door and throughout the civilized world. It smells in here like Vulcan's acrid forge, updated to encompass brake fluid, antifreeze. Light-headed Baxter hasn't eaten since he left the house. He's taste-testing saliva as Bob, with a wincing grin, ushers him under the shadow of his Mirage. He squints over his Salem at Baxter, who wants to recoil at facial evidence of a life lived with no expectation of quarter or remission. "Here's your noise source," Bob says, a matter of plain fact, shining his lamp on a pinhole-sized hole in the muffler.

The muffler.

"No pipes?" blurts Baxter, like one unfamiliar with the concept of tempting fate.

"Be back for pipes in spring," says Bob. Funny look in his bloodshot eye. Smug? Sympathetic? Wry? No matter.

While cowgirlish Sandy updates his paperwork, Baxter notes the others—passive pink and aggressive brown both—look older, worn, as if they've just observed at close range a person hammered into the ground by a pile driver. What could make these women alike, so hollow eyed and skittish (for Lemon-Lime, a relative improvement, since Snakeneck now looks about equally spooked)? That news flash! The shout show's been muted, audio replaced by Mantovani, stringy "Girl from Ipanema" washing over them all like a lobotomy. Whether that idiot boy, safe and smiling in seatbelt and scarf, knows it or not, something in the wide world's gone desperately wrong. But Sandy, chipper as ever, hands over a dot-matrix receipt—bottom line, no dollars, no cents—and a re-issued warranty on golden fake vellum. "There you go," she says, "something for nothing."

He *will* be back in the spring for pipes—and at summer's end for more pipes, and (because he'll hose off corrosives no more faithfully than he's ever done) next winter for yet more pipes (and another muffler thrown in for good measure like the loss leader it is, lollipop for seeing the dentist), before this car bites the dust for reasons more profound than exhaust; of all this Baxter has no doubt—but for now, for the next ten, twenty, sixty minutes, he is a man insanely content with life.

He looks on as that guy Bob lays acetylene on the joint where muffler meets pipe, glows gold in a molten-metal shower of his own making, a gaudy fireworking celebration of elemental matter and technique, of giving a sucker an even break, living up to promises, doing something useful in the world. Watching Bob work, Baxter sniffs and wells up, wonder drug notwithstanding. Holy shit, he thinks, an epiphany. If, in the glory of that moment, torch tossed spark into tank and the whole place went up in a Hollywood fireball, Baxter isn't a hundred percent sure how much he'd mind.

Brian Slattery

Here I am in my Underoos, in front of my grandmother's house. I was not a modest child.

Brian Slattery was raised in Upstate New York and now lives in New York City. He is twenty-six years old; this is his first published story.

BRIAN SLATTERY
The Things that Get You

*I*n the photograph, Neil and Roger are standing up to their calves in mud. Roger's shirt and shorts are stiff with dirt, rain, and blood; Neil is wearing a tank top and gym shorts that appear new, as if age and abuse are afraid of them, afraid of their wearer. They're both giving smiles, gigantic, cartoony, and Neil brings conviction to his by holding his arms out from his sides like he's more muscular than he is. Roger's arms hang, dragging his shoulders into a slouch, and scrutiny shows fans of darkness under his eyes. The picture was taken in Venezuela a few kilometers from the Brazilian border. They were faking their smiles because, after two weeks and twenty-six cases, eighteen terminal, the disease they were investigating still mystified them, and Roger looked so fatigued because, in a matter of days, he would exhibit its symptoms.

That was forty-two years ago, and Roger, now sixty-seven, examines the photograph in the den of the small house he shares with Katherine, his wife of twenty-nine years. The afternoon light, passing in stripes through the shutters, exercises yellow across the room: bands of yellow on the carpet, a yellow sheen on the bookcases; a swath of light igniting dust in the air that falls on Roger as he holds the photograph, which he has taken from the wall; a needle of shine on his fingernail, as his finger moves across the photograph's surface.

"You seem tired," Katherine says in bed one night. "Why can't you sleep?"

"I don't know," he says. A lie.

He met Neil Swanson in medical school, when Neil wore square wireframe glasses and Roger was still plump from college. Roger excelled because of his hands, hands that moved over the cadaver in gross anatomy like a satellite seen moving across the sky, steady, unerring; and because of his brain, made to hold and organize facts by the millions. Neil excelled because he was brilliant. He comprehended at once the mechanics of the body in relation to its environment, he could pull theory and structure from the barest facts with precision and childlike confidence, the kind that doesn't see its own genius. Near the end of second year, Neil told Roger that Roger was the smartest man he knew; and Roger paused, flattered, incredulous, suffocated in envy. Neil, every sentence you say reorders my brain. Neil, you don't know how stupid you make me feel.

Morning grows pink and orange in the small house, and Katherine moves through it with dry steps. She makes coffee; she makes sausage with cottage cheese. Roger watches from the table and marvels at her, his old girl, but she gives him a look that suggests confusion, that hints at fear.

"Do you want grapefruit juice?" she says.

"No. Not today."

"You used to like grapefruit juice. When we first met, you drank a gallon and a half of grapefruit juice a day. You said it improved your circulation and cleaned out your urethra."

"I said that?"

"Oh, yes," she says, "on our second date you said that."

The early days of their relationship are a carousel to him now, a rotation of restaurants and bars, trains and motels, a smear of color and sound, watery and strained music, and afterward, the sensation that he'd had a really good time coupled with a vague nausea. Neil was teaching at Johns Hopkins by then. Roger told him nothing of Katherine in his letters, would tell nothing until they were engaged. I'm getting married, he would say to Neil, come to our wedding and be my best man. Katherine and I have known each other only five months but it seems like a great idea. Please don't leave me.

In Venezuela, the disease sent sorties into Roger that he could not feel, spies that planted treachery in his body. They hid in his muscles, they hid in his bones, his lungs, his kidneys. Then all at once they struck: the aging king on a dusty throne was surrounded by assassins who pressed knives into his weakened flesh, began to torture him piece by piece, without revealing who had sent them, or why.

For two weeks Roger lay smoldering on a cot pulled from branches and strips of tires. He drank water from a rancid sponge; he ate manioc boiled and stirred into a thin slurry. Faces of caretakers drifted before him, they explained to Neil in Spanish that Roger was withering like the others, yes, the telling rash, yes, the boils raised on the skin. Days oozed into each other, a hot sludge of hours. And then:

"Roger, wake up."

Night. Voices of birds and small mammals from the trees. The wire frames above him in slashing clarity, the sharp lines of his lips, the dry cool of his hand on Roger's chest.

"You shouldn't touch me, Neil . . ."

"Roger, it's three in the morning and everyone is asleep. Animals are moving in the woods and we lost another patient. They buried him in the forest under a stone. Roger, I've woken you up to tell you that you're not going to die from this."

". . . what about liver cancer?"

"Maybe later, but not this, not now."

"Why not."

"Because you're too smart to die without knowing what got you."

Neil, Neil. Through his shirt he could feel the joints on the fingers of that cool hand, their weight on his scorched lungs, his frantic heart. In a hospital in Caracas, they pumped him with antibiotics, beating back secondary infections so his immune system could identify, surround, and destroy the intruders. Blue walls, a blur of nurses coming and going, doctors coming and going, but always Neil's face in vivid focus, Neil's hand laid on his chest. In the yellowing light of afternoon, the photograph off the wall in his hands, Roger can still see this, still feel this, as if he is sick again in that dark hut and Neil has come with medicine to save him.

"Something is eating holes in our zucchini." Katherine says. She has gardening tools, cloth gloves on her hands with dirt shoved into every stitch.

"What kind of holes?"

"Round straight holes."

"Maybe we're being attacked by a worm with fused vertebrae."

"Worms don't have vertebrae. I think someone's shooting arrows into our food at night. Arrows or darts."

"Maybe it's the Northern California pebble shrew."

"There's no such animal."

"There is."

"Do you still love me?"

"Of course I do."

She does not understand it, how Neil's death affected him. In this way, her life has been unfair to her. By the time Katherine met Roger, his friendship with Neil had become something rare. There was the work in Venezuela, which led to positions for both of them at the Centers for Disease Control. There was the long series of co-authored papers,

Neil's brilliance supported by Roger's balanced, almost flaw-
less methodology. They presented their work at conferences,
had papers published in books, published books that became
classics of the discipline. Years in the field, years in the lab.
Swanson and Smith. They used to joke that it sounded like a
duo that wrote musicals, that performed magic tricks. I am
the straight man, Roger used to think. I build the ground, I
lay down stones. You are the one who builds cathedrals, you
are the one who fashions flying machines from splinters and
string that drag us all into the sky, laughing and screaming in
terror.

Katherine did not meet Neil until the wedding, saw him
only seven times in her life, and she was not privy to the
stream of letters running between Maryland and California.
Eleven years ago—three before he died—Neil visited them
for four days at their house. She remembers him as a small,
quiet man, easy and understated. She did not catch the tor-
rent of information that raged between Neil and her husband, from the moment the two men caught sight of each
other in the airport until they dropped him off in front of the
terminal ninety-eight hours later; through every meal,
through all the strenuous walks along the water below the dry
cliffs; even while they reclined in lawn chairs side by side in
the backyard, the two men skinny and shirtless, reading
through sunglasses without speaking.

"No, Roger. Do you really still love me?"

"Yes. Yes."

There was no death scene between them; there was a phone
call. Roger in bathing trunks on a stool in the kitchen, Neil's
voice crackly and raspy over the phone, speaking from bed. I
can put in my own IV, Neil said. I administer my own shots.
They spoke then of conferences, they spoke of Venezuela, of
that town down there with mud streets and houses warped by
shifting earth, livestock running mad. They spoke of the two

streets that run parallel to each other and bear their names, Camino Swanson, Camino Smith, stretching from one end of town to the other, the names of the men who saved them from death. The weather here is terrible, Neil said. It has been hot, oppressive, then it rains so hard you can't breathe outside, then hot, oppressive all over again. Worse than Venezuela. You should have come out here, Roger said. No way, Neil said.

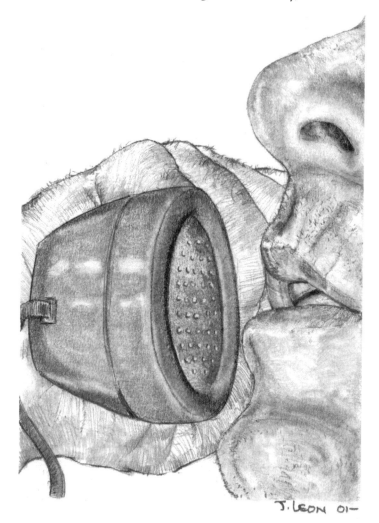

There was no drama in that. But when Neil died, Roger thinks, they went in and installed a device on my heart that put a cap on its activity, a limit. No. They moved my heart from its place in my chest and enclosed it in a room with barren walls, a plain wooden floor, a plain wooden ceiling. You can feel this much but no more, they said. This much can you give to your relatives. This much can you give to your wife, who loves you and whose love will continue to grow beyond your capacity to match it. We're sorry; it was an emergency procedure. They built the room to save me and left me there; and I want to leave it, but I think it may kill me if I do.

How to explain this to her? In a few years, she will go, or I will go, and then what? What is left for the one who stays? What name can you give it so it does not kill you? People should understand the things that get them. Heart attacks, liver failure. Scarlet fever, malaria, pancreatic cancer. A puncture wound through the lungs, asphyxiation, drowning. A brain hemorrhage, blood loss, from a buck knife through the skull, an accident with horses. Evisceration in a train wreck. These are the ways that heroes, victims, and family members go. It is the way that Neil went. They are dignified, they are sad, they are tragic; for them you can put words in medical files, obituaries, and eulogies; you can carve them into headstones like they did in ancient times and in the Old West, words to say when you speak of the one who is gone.

But this. Where are the words for this?

He moves toward his wife and brings her into his arms, repeating yes, yes, of course I do, of course, and she grows smaller, the bristles retract, as though she believes him. And that night, he sits up in bed and stares at the moonlight wavering through the shutters and across the bedspread, and he rambles to her about Neil and medical school and the things the two of them used to say to each other, and about how sorry he is that he's not capable of more; he begs her to understand, he begs her to forgive him for not being more than he is; but she is asleep for all of it, and does not mention it in the morning.

VERY SHORT FICTION AWARD
1st-, 2nd-, and 3rd-Place Winners

First-place winner: BRIAN SLATTERY
Brian Slattery receives $1200 for his first-place story, "The Things that Get You," which begins on page 153, preceded by his profile on page 152.

Second-place winner: SALLY SHIVNAN
Sally Shivnan receives $500 for "Something, Anything." Her fiction has appeared in journals including Glimmer Train *and* So to Speak, *and the* Washington Post *has featured her travel writing. She is also the proud parent of a couple of as-yet-unpublished novels. She teaches at University of Maryland, Baltimore County.*

"Something, Anything"
Every time I close my eyes, all I see is that damn mattress. I have never been able to understand why nobody thinks to tie those things fore-and-aft. Think for one blessed moment where the wind comes from when you're driving forward in a straight line on a freeway.

Third-place winner: SIMON VAN BOOY
Simon Van Booy receives $300 for "Snow Falls, and Then Disappears." He is twenty-six and from Britain. He likes surfing, classical music, painting, dogs, and the New York Giants. He has published stories and poetry in magazines and news-papers, and is the author of a collection of short stories entitled Love and the Five Senses, *which will appear in the spring. He lives on the east end of Long Island.*

"Snow Falls, and Then Disappears"
My wife is deaf. Once she asked if the snow made a sound when it fell, and I lied. We have been married twelve years today and I am leaving her.

We invite you to our website (www.glimmertrain.com) to see a listing of the top twenty-five winners and finalists. We thank all entrants for sending in their work.

Brad Barkley

This is me about age eight or so, happily trying out the new stilts my father had made for me. The stilts were part of a cycle of vaguely life-threatening toys I owned as a child, including a pogo stick, spring-loaded moon shoes, and, my favorite, a giant wooden spool of the type used to store electric cable. I would climb onto the spool and use my feet to propel it, rolling backward and forward through the streets, waving to neighbors, like a trained bear in the circus.

Brad Barkley is the author of a short-story collection entitled *Circle View*, and a novel, *Money, Love*, published by Norton in July of 2000. His stories have appeared in *Glimmer Train*, the *Oxford American*, the *Southern Review*, the *Georgia Review*, and the *Virginia Quarterly Review*, which awarded him the Balch Prize for best fiction. He has won writing fellowships from the Maryland State Arts Council and the National Endowment for the Arts.

BRAD BARKLEY

Another Perfect Catastrophe

 *odeo tricks*

We're cruising Dickson Street in the ragged vinyl buckets of my Pinto, and Sugar is chattering around a mouthful of peaches, telling me I'd better back up, he has just spotted a beret. I keep driving.

"Reed, you have to stop," he says. "Think of Bobby Seale, Sergeant Barry Sadler. Hey, Pablo *Picasso*, man." He tosses his fruit cup out the window, steals a Camel off the dash. "You saw it, right?" he says. I nod, sigh, pull over and brake. Already he is hovering at low-middle on my happy-with-him gauge because he has again made us late picking up Lyndsey at the Hen House, and the back wheels of my Pinto are scraping from the weight of the acetylene tanks he buys to make more of his large, homely sculptures. His words, not mine—he likes to say he is of the large-homely school. He welds the sculptures without ceasing, finishes one and starts the next, lets them rust away in the basement, in the attic, scattered around the yard.

So we're late and I'm torn because a feed cap is one thing, but this one really is a French beret, dark blue and new looking, which you have to admit is not something you see on the street every damn day. So I back up, wait for traffic to thin. We sit while the radio bounces out an old Donna Summer tune, then a commercial for the Hairport. The road empties and I throttle up again, hear the shush of wind and pavement as Sugar swings open the door, leans out—just beyond his knees the sidewalk blurs past and he is muffle-voiced, yelling, *A little left, Reed, a little left*, then reaches and snags the beret, bare knuckles an inch from the asphalt. Dirt and styrofoam whip around the floorboards. I ease back into traffic.

"Man, we nailed that sonofabitch," he says, slams the door, pries gum from the beret, and all I can see is Lyndsey and the several ways she gets irritated, twirling her hair, shaking her wrist so her watch slides down, chewing her lip. She is all about promptness. She expects things to be on time. Sugar slaps dust from the beret, tries it on. He tilts the rearview to check himself. Except for underwear, he never washes the clothes he finds before he wears them, and thank god underwear is a rarity. Mostly it is shoes, hats, T-shirts, the odd pair of pants. His latest T-shirt, minus a sleeve, advertises the Westmar High Girl's Field Hockey Team. The back says, *Girls Kick Butt!* He found it along Route 36, on the way home from the parts yard. He won't drive because of his logging leg (he calls it), which has hobbled him going on twelve years now. I don't mind, so Lyndsey minds for both of us, but what she would never let herself admit is that it was truly a righteous grab, that I never let the needle dip under 15 mph, that to someone watching we looked better than any rodeo trick rider, better than Tex Ritter or Monty Hale hauling a woman into the saddle. Lyndsey doesn't know these names. None of the movies she likes feature horses or gunplay.

I check my watch. "We missed Lyndsey," I say. "She's home by now and way pissed."

He fans his smoke out the window. "Hey, really, it's my bad, and I'll tell her that."

"I think she knows that, Sugar," I tell him. He nods, adjusts his beret. It covers the bald spot in his greying red hair.

"You need to marry that woman," he says. "All signs indicate that this is your last chance. And she's a good one, Reed, so don't blow it."

"I know," I say. The back wheels scrape. "I'm trying not to."

the generation gap

What I don't say is that *he* is the biggest chance that I will blow it. And you can't blame Lyndsey, can you? Sugar and I are thirty-five, the both of us, Siamese twins joined at high-school vandalism. Lyndsey is twenty-three, and I remember what that felt like: how you hit the exit door of state college and the ink on your diploma is still moist, and you feel like you can step along the next forty-some years without the least stumble if only you are bright enough to avoid any deep woods and keep to the bread-crumb trail that runs from your dorm room to the nursing home, about eight feet away. A few years will show you that the ones who tossed those crumbs ahead of you are only parents, bosses, teachers—all manner of fallible fuck ups. But at twenty-three you don't know that yet. There's your generation gap, in eight words or less. Not the Lilith Fair or websites or nose piercings or sexual stamina or hair loss. Only that chasm in understanding. What else you don't know at twenty-three is that if you hurl yourself down that path, along the way all you will ever find is what everybody else has found before you; all you will see is a tree stump in a glass case, the rings labeled year by year.

At home Lyndsey is shoving chairs and a coffee table around the room, rearranging the house that Sugar's parents gave him when they retired to Puerto Rico. Last month she repainted everything. The house is out away from town down a dirt road, which is a good thing given the pipe bombs, but lately Lyndsey has been showing me photos of split levels and two-car garages in the weekly real-estate circular. Cul-de-sacs, planned communities, etc. She would like to have neighbors, bushes, fluoride in the water, backyard barbecues—all the normalcy she missed out on growing up. She shops for houses on the internet.

Lyndsey has put the dog out in the yard, tethered to the clothesline, and I watch through the window while Sugar unloads his acetylene tanks and rolls on the grass with the dog in the cold, then walks around looking at his latest sculpture, which he is making from tractor parts and the soup cans he blows into shards. He blows things apart, then welds them back together, and this makes in those sculptures a kind of tension I like, even though I do not much care for midnight blasts and the big balls of flame he sends into the tree tops. The dog is a bloodhound named Ernest, who Sugar found and named (drunk, he will try to explain this) after *The Importance of Being Earnest*, saying that he didn't think Oscar Wilde would mind the borrowing or the misspelling, and that, anyway, Mr. Wilde shouldn't have taken the title, as it would have been, with the altered spelling, perfect for Ernest Hemingway's autobiography. I may be confusing the story, but somehow out of it all he managed to name a dog. He used to have a goldfish named Wuthering Heights, and a mynah bird named Absalom, Absalom.

The dog knows how to sniff out money, the way airport dogs can sniff drugs. Sugar bought a training manual and educated the dog to find greenbacks, paper money. He will turn him loose in the neighborhood, and on a good day Ernest will bring home a few singles and sometimes a five or a ten. We have no idea where he finds them, only that he is determined to find them and does. This for Lyndsey is exploitation, and she has a fervent sympathy for animals, in the manner of all people who have at some time or another been gravely disappointed by human beings. When I met her she was VP of the local PETA chapter, and even once stood with others downtown across from Vogel's Furs, naked under a blanket with a sign indicating she would rather be naked than wear fur, which would be my preference for her as well, if you could separate the politics from the nakedness. Which of course you never can. We argued about this right after she moved in last August. I took the position that training a dog to hunt money is not even in the neighborhood with meat eating and fur wearing, but when you are a twenty-three-year-old graduate student in finance, your thirty-five-year-old construction-supervisor boyfriend is pretty much wrong on everything. So we avoid the subject. I do love her.

It has grown cold, early November, and I head out with Lyndsey to split wood in the backyard. Sugar is under the carport, his torch fired up and sending down a waterfall of orange and white. He limps as he walks around the sculpture, looking for the next place to spot weld a shard of soup can. Lyndsey has on one of my old flannels over her blue jeans, with leather gloves cinched tight around her wrists. The girl can cut some wood, keeps her hair tied back. If you ever want to fall in re-love with your POSSLQ, let her wear flannel and do hard work. I watch her a while, stack the wood, take the sledge and wedge when she tires and we trade. Sugar hammers on his sculpture, the sound ringing through the cold.

"You pretty much trust him, don't you?" Lyndsey says. She wipes sweat from her face with her sleeve.

"What do you mean?" I say, though I know exactly where she is headed with this.

"Well, he's over there using a hammer, a torch. He isn't setting himself on fire, he isn't getting killed."

"Thanks for the update."

"You don't have to take care of him, Reed."

"I know that."

"You do and you don't. I think you feel guilty about him,

and you know that's not healthy."

When she starts using words like *healthy*, it's usually time to let the argument drop. I swing the sledge, miss, say nothing.

"We could move out of here and you'd still be his friend. I would too. We don't have to *stay* here."

I swing again, lay the wood open and wet. "Listen, I like living here. We don't pay any rent. Sugar is a good guy." I shrug. If you want your language to fail, try explaining your male friends to your female mate.

"What is it you *do* all day with him? I mean, besides dig clothes out of trash dumpsters?" I work only six months of the year, during heavy construction season. The rest of that time is down time, nothing time, which I would not trade for anything.

"The street," I tell her. "Sugar would never go diving some dumpster. He says that fate hands him his wardrobe." She knows all of this and only uses reminding as a way of shaming me with the details. When she first met Sugar she went right along, saying that he made her laugh. Sugar has always been like a big toy, and when the batteries finally go, most are done with him. He gets old, Sugar does.

"Yeah, fate hands him most everything else, too," Lyndsey says. She adjusts her bra strap. "You're both too young to just quit your lives."

Sugar leaves his carport and starts walking around the yard, within earshot. We fall quiet, but I know this argument has only gone underground for a while. Sugar has his welding helmet tipped open, and is walking around in circles studying the ground as though surveying it. Say what you like, the boy *does* have plans in his head.

He walks over toward us, smiles at Lyndsey. She used to say he was handsome before his bothersomeness erased it. The welding helmet hangs over his face like part of some bird costume. The helmet, when he found it (on Industrial Boulevard, leaning against a mattress), was missing its dark eye guard, so Sugar glued in a square of blue plastic cut from a soda bottle. The plastic leaves his vision wavered, like standing in the deep end, but he claims this makes for good sculpture.

I motion toward the carport. "What're you working on?" I know the answer already.

He shrugs. The helmet falls down and he pushes it up again. "New sculpture. *A Perfect Catastrophe*, I call it."

I grin at him. This is an old joke. All of his sculptures, since the start, have had the same title, only with different numbers.

"Another *Perfect Catastrophe*," I say. "I've lost count."

"Fifty-seven," he says. Lyndsey looks back and forth between us as if we are speaking in some elaborate code, which, I guess, we are.

"Hey, Reed, I need some lumber," Sugar says. "I mean I ordered some and need to go get it. I need a ride."

Lyndsey turns and shoots me a look, one of those little signals of anger or lust that will make of us finally a couple.

"How soon?" I ask him.

He laughs. "Hey, it's like that old joke. You know, guy says I need a board, salesman says how long, guy says a long time, I'm building a house."

I laugh with him, at the joke and at the way he compresses every joke, his life, everything in it compressed, hurrying toward nothing.

economics 101

That night in the bedroom, Lyndsey practices tai chi. She does Needle at Sea Bottom and Waving Hands Like Clouds. This relaxes her and focuses her both, she says, much the way TV-beer does me. I do remote control and Doritos while I watch her. I hate to be predictable, but I go with what works. On Friday nights I watch Lyndsey on the eleven o'clock news, when she does the Wall Street Wrap-Up, three minutes of local stocks and investing tips sandwiched between the weather and sports. I like how she seems on TV, so distant and so much there all at once. I like how dressed up she is, her hair and makeup done, and how smart, talking all of us through graphics of the Dow and NASDAQ. She gave me another little signal to watch for, and some Fridays (not every), just when she says, "Back over to you, Bill," she gives a little twitch of a smile, and then her full-kilowatt blast right behind it. Wouldn't see the twitch if you weren't looking for it. That little gesture is for me, to say that she is thinking about me and loves me, right there with the camera and half of Hagerstown eyeing her. I bend close to the TV every Friday to watch, and if she does it, I shout like I have just won the state lottery.

Right now she is moving in slow motion, doing White Crane Spreads Wings. She is half-naked as she practices, wearing blue sweat pants, her hair still wet from the shower. She told me once that she is locating her internal self, her centeredness, that tai chi means "the grand, ultimate fist." I wonder at this, how she finds her center by making her insides a fist. She grew up with a father who lost jobs the way other people lose car keys, and a mother convicted eighteen times for shoplifting. I would make my innards a fist too, I think.

I watch her in the dark, lit by the blue of the TV, her nakedness in the cold light, her slow movements like storm clouds in a nature film. She hates the TV, but right now it renders her beautiful. After finishing with Fair Lady Works At Shuttles, she sits on the bed beside my knees, points the remote at the wall behind me, and turns off the tube, a decent bank shot. She clicks on the light. We are about to talk.

"We need to talk," she says. From atop her computer she lifts one of the green ledger books she uses in her Investment Management course, opens it across the bed.

"Here's the plan, Reed. If we move out of here, into some student ghetto until I graduate, then we pay out three-hundred a month that we aren't paying now."

I nod, look at her. "Three hundred in the hole. Okay."

"But—" She kneels across from me. "If we're near campus we cut out my commuting costs, and you are closer to town. We don't have to drive Sugar anywhere at all, and we don't have to pay for his food. Conservatively, this saves us maybe a hundred and fifty."

"But still in the hole," I tell her.

"Right, but what do we get for our hundred and fifty? We get us, honey. We get to *be* with each other, instead of tiptoeing around and acting polite and making sure we have on our bathrobes."

As she says this, I look down at the rows of credits and debits written in blue ink in her neat hand, then upward, at the way the wet tips of her hair sway and lightly brush her nipples. All in all, it's a convincing argument.

"I've lived here a long time, Lyndsey. Eleven years is a long time."

She takes my hands, knee-walks over her own ledger book as she moves forward to straddle my thighs.

"Listen," she whispers, "you aren't doing him any good by staying here. He needs to find something else. His own life, maybe, instead of just tagging along with yours. You don't have to stay."

"Yeah, but what's wrong with staying? We have privacy."

"I would just like a little *normalcy* for once, Reed."

I start to speak, then we both jump as Sugar detonates another pipe bomb from the backyard. Orange light bursts against the curtain a half-second before the explosion rattles my keys on the dresser. Then I hear the shards of soup can hit the driveway. Lyndsey closes her eyes, draws steady breaths through her nose. I squeeze her hand.

"Let me think about it," I say.

She nods. "Better think hard."

how we met

Friday nights at the Hen House and all-you-can-eat crab legs. Snow crab legs, and Sugar wanted to eat them in the snow, in February. Lyndsey was our waitress ten Fridays running, and slowly became a shared joke, a persistent glance, a nudge in the ribs from Sugar. We were two men just off from work (well, me), tired, doughy enough to be harmless. We asked her one night in early spring and she went with us, riding. Her T-shirt had a cartoon of a hen with a fishing pole, reeling in a big catfish. She wore black shorts. Gave her my denim coat to wear in the Pinto with its bad heat, Sugar leaning up between the seats like our eight-year-old and we are on our way to Six Flags. We bought little pony bottles of beer along with handfuls of Ding-Dongs and Slim Jims, and rode out to the golf course, across the parking lot, right up onto the cart path beside the first tee, and clicked the Pinto down to parking lights. "I don't know about this, guys," she kept saying, and I drove slowly to reassure her, the cinders crunching beneath us, careful to stay on the path and not dig any tire ruts on the fairways. We handed our empties to Sugar and he placed them back in the carton. After a bit, Lyndsey settled into it, saying we were the most cautious vandals she'd ever seen. I liked the sound of her voice in the dark, the way her hair smelled like hush puppies.

Near dawn, the sky just edging toward light, we parked atop a hill beside the fourteenth green. Below us was the dark gape of a pond, the surface puckered by fish going after mosquitoes. Dew settled over the Pinto so that every few minutes I had to run the wipers. It was not yet sunrise, though there was a little rag of grey in the corner of the night, and the trees and yellow flags began to shape themselves. We got out of the car, walked to the edge of the hill in the wet grass, and below us the town laid spread out in darkness, the arc lamps strung like pearls through the streets. Light in the sky shifted again and all in one moment the street lights blinked out, as if the town were giving in to daylight. "Wait till you see this," I told Lyndsey, and I watched her watching the town. "One more minute," Sugar said, and we were quiet.

Right below, a few hundred yards under our shoes, was the John Deere plant, and when the light in the sky notched up again, the green and yellow of those tractors bloomed into being like a sudden field of dandelions. I took Lyndsey's chin and angled it down for her to see, the way Sugar did me the first time up there. Seventy-seven of them—tractors, harvesters, combines, backhoes, excavators—parked in neat rows on a wide gravel lot. Always seventy-seven, we had noticed through the years, so much so that we had stopped counting and went by faith. Dew glistened on the shiny green paint, the shadows of the machinery angled left in their own neat grey rows.

"Oh my god," Lyndsey whispered. She took my hand, then Sugar's.

I squeezed. "Like it?"

She nodded. "So beautiful. Like a Zen rock garden."

"With internal combustion," Sugar said. We stood silent and watching, as if we might see the little shift as the sun lifted over the hills and the shadows darkened and narrowed beneath the rows of machinery, as the town began to ripple with cars and noise. Then the sprinklers spread out over the fairways rose out of the ground and began spewing water in tapered arcs, and somewhere out over the fairways we heard a lawnmower start up.

"We better get moving," I said.

As we drove along the cinder paths, Lyndsey unpinned her name tag from her Hen House shirt and stuck it into my dash, left it there.

"I want to come back," she said. "I want to see that again."

why she stays
I don't know.

logging leg
It was something to do, road-trip up to Oregon for a
summer, escape the worst of the heat and no money. We were
twenty-three, same age Lyndsey is now. We signed on with
Hennesy Forestry Management, Inc. for six bucks an hour
plus free lunch off the back of the silver truck at the foot of
the logging road. We spent our nights in bars, chalking games
of dominos on the tables, trading money for half a buzz and a
few jukebox dances with the local women, pretending that a
pair of narrow beds and long hours of work equaled adventure. During the days we worked the skid trail, chainsawing
the downed trees into eight-foot lengths, walking across the
rows of logs under a high, dark canopy, with everything—the
air, the logs, the ground—soaked with moisture. Sugar
worked as a ballhooter, stepping across the logs, pushing them
with a pole hook into neat bundles. After two days we could
work in silence, the best way, speaking with only our eyes and
nods of the head. The trees columned upward under a sky
dark grey and marbled, the ground under our toe spikes
needled, leaved, soft.

One late afternoon, a Thursday, I motioned Gil to back up
the tractor to a bundle of logs and guided the winch while
Sugar stepped across and looped the choker cable around the
bundle. He looked at me to hit the winch, and as the motor
started grinding I stepped back with a pole hook to guide the
bundle into place. As I moved away I watched the rubber
bindings on Sugar's right boot come unstrapped, the spikes
left behind, stuck in the log, and his right foot slipping down

inside the choker just as the winch gathered the cable into its slow tightening. I looked at him as if seeing him there would tell me that nothing this wrong could possibly be happening. His eyes held me, his mouth open and words splitting out of him as I moved toward the winch to hit the shutoff, and saw the cable pull slowly through his jeans just above his knee. His other leg bicycled against the stack of wood and noise poured from his mouth, his hands grabbing at nothing. The cable insisted its way into his flesh, and I heard his bones as my hand found the red button, and Gil, white faced, exited the truck and clicked on his walkie talkie. I didn't move, could not move. Sugar's eyes held me. My own eyes, still new to this silent language of work, found no words to give him, and I looked away.

the tough questions

"Why are we still together?" I ask. Lyndsey is readying for the Hen House, and I watch her slip on a T-shirt, zipper her skirt. "I mean, why are you with me?"

She sighs. "How did you get this old and stay this dumb?"

I shrug. "Easiest thing I ever did."

She shakes her head, pulls on her Hen House sweatshirt. If she follows her plans, in two years she will be making four times what I make now. "Because I love you, Reed. The oldest reason there ever was."

"But why?"

"You aren't supposed to ask why about love. You're supposed to let it stay a mystery. That's the rule."

I nod and watch her clip her hair up to keep it out of the catfish filets and cole slaw. "Love isn't such a mystery, really."

She cuts her eyes at me. "No?"

"Not for me." I shrug. "A soft, warm body, a bed where we talk in the dark, your little TV smile on Friday night. Where's the big mystery?"

She shakes her head, frowns. "Well, that's shallow of you."

I know that she is no great believer in mystery either, that this is just something you say about love when you are twenty-three years old. Her parents held more mystery than most see in a lifetime, a dad shedding jobs almost weekly, a steady march of repossessors, and a mother who could not stop stealing eye makeup or cans of soup or 45s from the record store. Lyndsey turned away from all of that, left it for good at sixteen, and now every step of her existence is planned out—career, vacations, the life she wants with me. She left mystery a long time ago and has not looked back.

I look at her. "Why shallow? Who says love can't be made up of real things? If there is any mystery, then that's it: there isn't any."

She walks over, takes my chin in her fingers. "Try as hard as you can to make sense."

"Listen, you wonder about how we spend our days, let me tell you. A couple months ago I took Sugar out to a work site for copper scraps. One of the guys on the crew stole his friend's bag of Cheetos, just goofing around, and nailed it to the top of a frame post. Then all afternoon we sat and watched these two crows swoop down and land, pluck a Cheeto from the bag, and fly off with it. One by one, until it was empty."

She smiles. "That's pretty cool."

"The point is, Cheetos and crows are just things. But you can love them for themselves. What's wrong with just loving the thinginess of things? They don't have to *mean*."

She leans down, kisses my upper lip. "Like those tractors on the golf course."

I nod. What I don't say is that it was Sugar who first showed me the tractors, Sugar who made a dozen guys stop a day's work and sit in the shade to watch crows. Sugar is all mystery, and there is, I think, no solving him.

She ties her hair back. "Listen, pick me up at midnight, okay?"

"Okay."

"And bring Sugar with you. We'll go ride, just like old times. It'll make us all feel better. We'll see some thingy things."

"You're too young to have any old times," I say. She gives me a look. "Okay, Sugar and me, things, midnight."

the old times

Before we leave that night, I find Sugar in the backyard, smoking cigarettes in the cold, hammering nails.

"Where's the torch?" I ask him.

"Not tonight. Other plans. A wedding present, actually."

He is pounding two-by-sixes together into a big square. He tacks angle irons into the corners.

"Wedding present for who?" I say.

"For you, Reed, who else?"

"So I'm getting married? This is news to me, buddy."

He motions me to help, and we place the square of boards on an even spot in the backyard. Sugar tosses a plastic tarp across it. "I have eyes and ears, both, Reed. Don't tell me you aren't getting married. And you should, right?"

"That's my understanding, though I may have missed something." He hands me a staple gun and we walk around opposite sides of the wood frame, tacking the blue tarp to the boards. Above us the moon is thin and cold, the sky metal black. I feel sweat freeze in the hairs of my beard.

"Come on with me," I tell him. "Lyndsey wants to go for a ride. Like old times, she says."

He grins. "She isn't old enough—"

"I know, I told her that."

Ernest is watching us, his head lolling out of the doghouse Sugar made him from a yellow fertilizer barrel. Sugar finishes stapling and lays a bead of caulk over the staples.

"It's a little nippy for caulking," I tell him. He shrugs, says it will set eventually. He rubs his logging leg, which always bothers him more in the cold. We are quiet a minute.

"You ever think about it?" I glance down at his hand rubbing the knot on the side of his leg. "I mean, remember it?"

J. LEON 01

He peels caulk off his fingers. "I got three roommates, Reed. You, Lyndsey, and that memory. Every morning I wake up, it's there at the breakfast table eating Cap'n Crunch."

I nod, take a breath. "I didn't do everything I could have then. You know? I didn't... act." We stand together, looking at the tarp-covered box in the middle of the yard.

"What was there to do, a thing like that?" He shrugs. "A long time ago, Reed. I never held you to any blame. Things go the way they go."

The tarp ripples in a cold wind. Sugar picks up his welding helmet and puts it on, tips the mask up.

"You gonna tell me what this is?" I ask him. "Another perfect catastrophe?"

He smiles. "For a wedding present? Not a chance. It's a surprise, for both of you." While I am warming the Pinto, I see him with the garden hose pointed at this thing he has just built, as if he is washing off the plastic tarp, washing away all his hard work.

We get Lyndsey on time this go around, and have already been to the 421 for pony beers and Slim Jims and Ding Dongs. We find our way to Green Valley golf course and find the cart paths chained off, a security guard's car parked next to the clubhouse.

"Well, damn," Sugar says. "Somebody ruined it for us."

"Where to?" I ask.

"Just drive around," Sugar says. "Just cruise and eat and drink."

Lyndsey shakes her head. "I don't want to just drive around all night." Her Hen House pin is still in my dash, where she stuck it five months ago.

"Why not?" Sugar says.

"I know a place," I tell them.

I drive us over to the giant parking lot behind Burlington

Industries, where in the summer the tennis hacks line up to pound balls against the big concrete slab at the back of the lot. We scale the wall from its tapered end and sit in the high middle of it, our legs dangling, asphalt twenty feet below us. Behind us is the big steel and glass building with its fountain spewing water up past the fourth floor. We are nearing Christmas, and the white lights in the fountain have been replaced by red and green ones, the mist blowing off the fountain, holding the color for a second, then vanishing into darkness.

Lyndsey wraps a blanket around her legs and scoots close to me, the hood of her coat edging her face with fake fur. We pass the little bottles of beer and fire up foul-smelling Swisher Sweets and sit in the cold drinking and smoking, not talking, Sugar pushing the mask of his welding helmet up and down so that the hinges squeak.

"You ever think about doormen?" Sugar says. He says this from behind the mask, his voice muffled. "I mean it's weird. Say you're at that job for forty years. That is forty years of doing a single thing eight hours a day: opening and closing that one door."

I nod. "Yeah, strange. After that much time you must develop a relationship with that door. You know how many seconds it takes to swing closed, how much it weighs, what it smells like, where all the little nicks are in the wood." I feel Lyndsey shivering beside me. She finishes her second beer and opens a third, reaches for my cigar and holds it in her mittened hand, puffing and coughing, like a cartoon of someone smoking. Sugar is not done with doormen yet.

"I mean," he says, "that would be the worst part, that after you're seventy years old you look back and that's what you can say about your life. 'Well, I opened that door a lot.' Like, that's the whole ball of wax. That would be death to me, a job like that."

"At least it's a job," Lyndsey says. "At least you know what you're doing the next day." I give her hand a squeeze, open another beer for her.

"What would be the worst way to die?" I ask them. "Aside from being a doorman, I mean. I vote drowning."

"No *way*," Lyndsey says. "Burning up in a fire. Think how much a little arm burn on the toaster hurts."

"But it's quick," Sugar says. "The worst would be falling, like from a plane. All that time down and down and down, knowing what's coming, thinking about all the ways you fucked up."

"You wouldn't have time to think," Lyndsey says. "You'd be panicking."

I shake my head. "There is always time to think, no matter what."

"Hell, yes," Sugar says and tips up his mask. "Watch this." He stands up, wobbles, stretches his arms out, then jumps off the high wall toward the parking lot below, his loose jacket fluttering up behind him. Half a second later he lands on both feet and his mask clanks shut. Then he limps around in a fast circle, saying, *Damn, damn, damn,* over and over, a fast little song.

"Nice going," I tell him. "You could've broken your stupid leg."

He smiles. "Just proving my point. All the way down, I thought about the pastrami sandwich I had for lunch."

Lyndsey lets out a sound that is half laugh, half disgust. "Yeah, and that's about as deep as your thinking would go, too." The way she shakes her head, I can tell she is drunk. With a small, thoughtless motion of her wrist, she throws down her little beer bottle and it smashes on the pavement next to Sugar, pieces splintering across the asphalt. For a second, we are held in silence, as if waiting to see which way this moment will turn. Lyndsey looks at me, looks away.

"Missed me," Sugar says. His voice echoes around the parking lot, disappears up into the dark with the red and green mist behind us. He grins. "Strike one," he says. Lyndsey smiles at him, lifts another from the cardboard pack and wings it out into the dark, spinning, wind whistling at its neck. Sugar backs up, eyeing it, then snaps his neck so the welding mask swings down and he lets the bottle hit him full in the face, the glass shattering off the hard angles of the mask and spilling shards into his clothes.

"Man oh man," Sugar says, voice muffled. "Again."

Lyndsey lifts, tosses, and Sugar leans back, letting the bottle hit and smash over him, a tiny popping sound, the pieces falling away from him as he moves.

"Reed, I kid you not," he says, "you have to try this."

I look at Lyndsey. "Go on if you want to," she says.

I stand, jump, take the shock in my frozen legs. Sugar slips the mask over my head. It smells like copper pennies and sweat. I tip up the mask, look at Lyndsey framed in the red and green mist. "Don't kill me," I tell her.

She smiles. "Make sure it hits the mask, not your head." She flings another bottle out against the sky and I watch it as far as I can and then at the last second close my eyes and hear it glance off the left side of the mask, skitter on the pavement.

"Good try," Sugar says.

"Not good," I say. "I cheated, blinked." I look at Lyndsey. "Again."

She takes careful aim on me, and the glint of the glass, her halo of fine hair, the red-green mist behind her are all filtered blue, like I have found my own deep end. A brief knife-glint of bottle in the night sky, a wave of indigo, then the *pop* against the face plate and bits of light splintering around me, like I am falling away from the world or being launched from it. Lyndsey waves in my vision, arm raised, and then she lets fly again in a line drive. I keep my eyes open, move my legs, let another bottle smash against the iron over my face and explode into stars. Behind me I hear Sugar cheering me, and Lyndsey stands at the edge of the wall with another bottle in hand. A girl who loves me, who wants to make her insides a fist, and as she flings and misses she bobbles, half a second, at the edge of that wall, and throws her arms up and out to catch back her balance, and holds there, framed in a blue-white mist like some Orion or Cassiopeia seen through fog. And I know how much this girl needs *us*, as much as she wants only me. In Lyndsey's way of wanting, there will be no room for Sugar or bad parents, no accidental trips or falls, no mystery or blowing things apart—only a life as predictable as gravity.

This is not ancient history, not the days of chasing clothes along curbs and gutters or the days of the logging leg and the nights of weary bones, and the red button I could never quite push enough. This is Lyndsey, this is love blasted into shards that filter down through me. I lift the mask away and it squeaks and the cold pushes in behind it. I look up at her, and she raises the next pony bottle and promises it will hurt plenty without the mask, swears at herself for almost falling, and I stop her cold.

"You want to get married?" The words bounce around the asphalt.

She looks. Blinks. Shrugs. "Do you?"

Sugar stands beside me, pulling glass out of my clothes. I nod at Lyndsey, slip the mask off to put her back in this world. "Yeah," I tell her, "it sounds like a plan."

She sets the last empty back in the carton, wraps her arms around herself. "Okay then."

Sugar takes back his mask, slides it on, tips it up. "If you give the present," he says, "you create the event."

falling

That night we both fall into bed drunk and tired and cold, sleep arriving like some narcotic, and the last thing I hear before I give over to it is Sugar out in the backyard in fifteen-degree weather, spraying the garden hose again.

By the next evening Lyndsey is freaked out, because her eyes look like they should after the night we had, like they have been through a golf-ball washer, and she has the Wall Street Wrap-Up at 11:17, right after Stu Nelson with weather. But she mixes in enough excitement about rings and dresses and honeymoon to let me know that last night has not been filed under "Too Many Ponies."

She kisses me and heads out. I sit watching TV, downing the odd aspirin or two. A little while later Sugar walks out of the kitchen eating a powdered donut, his mouth ringed white. He hands me a shoebox, the ends duct taped. All day he has been in the carport hammering and welding, his face, even in this cold night, streaked with sweat. I open the box and find what look like two pairs of rollerskates, the old skate-key type meant to tighten to your sneakers. Sugar lifts them from the box, the worn leather straps tangled, and turns them over to show me where he has removed the metal wheels and welded in a pair of thin, iron blades running parallel. Ice skates.

"Your wedding present," he says. "And that's not all. C'mon." He leads me to the backyard, where the tiny rink he has fashioned from the boards and plastic tarp lies shining under a half moon, the ice uneven and puckered along its surface.

He pulls a skate key from his jeans pocket and we sit in the frosted grass to try on the skates. The eleven o'clock news has started, and soon it will be time to go inside, sit on the couch, and watch for that little twitch of a smile from Lyndsey. But for now we take to the ice. The rink is only about ten feet square, and we push around in small circles like we are chasing one another, the iron blades scraping up little white ribbons of ice. Then Sugar grips my hand and we begin to whip each other around, turning faster, nearly falling, the whole table of ice rocking slightly on the uneven ground. The wind blows an eddy of old snow off the roof of the house. We skate around in the pale moonlight, breathing the cold air, hands slippery with sweat, the silhouettes of all of Sugar's perfect catastrophes around us.

"I have to go soon," I tell him, out of breath. He nods, his face sweaty. Beneath us, the ice begins to crack from our weight, the underside shot through like shattered windshield glass. I think of breaking through into cold water, into the rush and press of a river, of how it would feel falling into all that blackness, the way it must have felt to Sugar in that moment when he knew that the log was no longer under his foot. But of course there is no river, no black water beneath us. The TV flickers blue against the curtains. Soon enough I will head inside to watch it, to warm up, to wait for her small signal. The ice rink splinters, pieces of it sliding across the surface, the larger chunks tripping us. The boards are loose, pulling apart. We keep skating as long as we can, the dead grass of winter pushed flat underneath us, the black November sky above us. All around the moon, a pale ring of ice glows, promising more snow.

The Last Pages

*Helga and Helmut Burmeister, new to
New York City, in 1928*

H. G. CARROLL

*U*pon waking, going to bed, in the shower, as he shaves, in his car, between mouthfuls, while loving, and clipping his toenails, as he scratches, without notice, he sings the boleros he hears—fugitive love songs of longing and loss; so tender, as if coming from an animal wounded by birth with a vital organ outside its body—so often and so out of tune, were he not so wrapped in it, even he could almost not bear it.

Photo credit: Stacy Rudy

ROBERT CHIBKA

*W*hen your novel makes clear that it intends to take its own sweet (and quite a bit more of your sour) time, and your stories have all been tending toward an awkardly novelettical forty to sixty pages, it's a very nice thing indeed to find one willing to be short. An inordinate pleasure, in fact, to complete one like "Muffler," which in turn concerns precisely the inordinate, irrational, insidious, and disproportionate power of pleasures and their opposites. My man Baxter, preferring to live his life at one remove, is so fortressed against melodrama's rollercoasting ups-'n'-downs that he's really in their thrall. This story is also a baleful reflection on the necessary sense of the familiar, predictable, typical ("As usual, as always, as ever...") that conditions expectations and actually generates the stories we can't help telling ourselves, endings we can't stop seeking, in muffler shops as it does in fiction.

188

BRAD BARKLEY

*T*his story came about when I was looking at old drafts that for one reason or another I'd never finished (most, it turned out, because they were dumb ideas, written as though I'd had half my brain tied behind my back). But this one was worth salvaging, I decided, if only I changed the main character's name and gave him a girlfriend. So I did that draft, and thought, yes, it's just about there, only get rid of that scene in the middle, and maybe just write one or two tiny new scenes—nothing earth shaking, mind you. This continued for a month or two, until I ended up with what you see here, which looks nothing like the original story at all. I think I salvaged maybe three words and a semicolon from the old version. It reminds me now of the joke I heard from some conceptual comedian, who said he had in his possession a valued family heirloom, an ax once owned by Daniel Boone himself. Of course, he said, his grandfather had lost the ax head in the river years ago and had to replace it, and then sometime later the ax handle broke and so a new one was added, but still...

J. M. FERGUSON

$\mathcal{I}$n the city where I live there is indeed a hole-in-the-wall espresso place which I've been walking to in the mornings, and there's also an animal shelter at the edge of town, if only semi-secluded. Most important, perhaps, there really was a sad and pensive stranger who appeared during my walks for a couple of months in the autumn of my life. He vanished abruptly, but if ever he reappears, I'd still like to buy him that cup of coffee he declined, if only to thank him for starting me thinking about and writing "Gleanings" before I knew where or if it was going, or even what to call it.

190

LOIS TAYLOR

*T*he uncanny part of writing for me has been the history of coincidences. Spooky, really. I was stuck halfway through the writing of a novel when I came upon one of Glimmer Train's *Writers Ask* issues and there it was: INSPIRATION/DISCIPLINE. Further, there were quotes by a novelist I was then reading. What could be clearer? I kept this pamphlet nearby and whenever I was stuck, I read it again. The novel got done. Writing for me has been beyond the loneliness you hear so commonly lemented; it is closer to corresponding via a set of drums. It's the practical stuff that helped—writers suggesting I read work out loud when I got stuck, or finish a day's work midsentence. I think writers crave such information. Much of the dailiness of the writing is more mysterious than the initiation rites of the Masons. I'm stunned when I learn that some writer I admire writes in longhand, or at night, and I ponder these facts long and hard. The story in these pages was begun fifteen years ago. When a story is truly finished, there is a feeling of not having another word to say on the matter. I also write poetry and the feeling there is very different, because the door to the poem always remains slightly ajar.

Lois Taylor

BRIAN SLATTERY

$\mathcal{T}$he banjo is a simple instrument. It is a wooden neck, a sliver of a bridge, a handful of pegs, a dowel, and a hoop of wood or metal with the skin of an animal stretched over it. If a banjo is broken, you can usually fix it with a screwdriver. Before bluegrass, they played the banjo with the thumb and the nail of the middle finger, no fingerpicks attached.

These are simple elements, monosyllables of music; but out of them, patterns of infinite complexity and variation emerge. Notes gurgle and warp, rhythms shift and dodge and weave. If someone really knows what he is doing on the banjo, you see only his right hand pivoting up and down, his hand sliding back and forth, but you hear a song wrapped around a deep groove, a pulsing, hypnotizing thing that grabs your feet, reaches into your gut, and makes you move. Someday, I hope I can write like that.

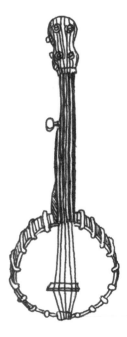

AMALIA MELIS

*A*fter I moved out of my parents' house I was snooping around in the basement and I found a book my grandmother used to learn English in night school after she came to the United States. Some of her answers had been penciled in. That got me thinking— what was she trying to do? Fit in? Understand the country she moved to? Forget the whitewashed houses she was not going to live in anymore?

So I started to write about what she might have felt. Perhaps I have done her justice with this story, perhaps I am completely off the mark. This is my version of events, and that is what stories are, anyway—the writer's interpretation of events. I do know that I am not finished writing about her yet.

Photo credit: Dimitris Mytaras

MONICA WOOD

I like endings. Because I take such care with them, every story I write feels like a closed universe. But after I wrote a story called "Ernie's Ark," in which I first discovered Ernie and Marie, something happened. The story nagged at me in funny ways—first in the form of a minor character, the code inspector who comes to Ernie's house to tell him to take down an ark he has built on his lawn. I couldn't stop wondering what that man must have been thinking, witnessing Ernie's strange compulsion. So I wrote a story in that man's voice, and it turned out he had a big family of brothers that was in tatters because the youngest brother had crossed the picket line at the paper mill. Which got me thinking about Ernie's son, and what kind of parents he and Marie might have been before they appeared to me in that first story. I turned back the clock twenty-five years and started writing "That One Autumn," one of nine stories that sprang from "Ernie's Ark," a story whose ending turned out— to my great surprise and glee—to be a beginning.

This is Pinky, who doesn't mind listening to crummy drafts.

$\mathscr{P}$AST CONTRIBUTING AUTHORS AND ARTISTS

Many of issues 1 through 41 are available for eleven dollars each.

Robert A. Abel • Linsey Abrams • Steve Adams • Susan Alenick • Rosemary Altea • Julia Alvarez • Brian Ames • A. Manette Ansay • Margaret Atwood • Kevin Bacon • Aida Baker • Russell Banks • Brad Barkley • Kyle Ann Bates • Richard Bausch • Robert Bausch • Charles Baxter • Ann Beattie • Barbara Bechtold • Cathie Beck • Jeff Becker • Janet Belding • Sallie Bingham • Kristen Birchett • Melanie Bishop • James Carlos Blake • Corinne Demas Bliss • Valerie Block • Joan Bohorfoush • Harold Brodkey • Danit Brown • Kurt McGinnis Brown • Paul Brownfield • Judy Budnitz • Christopher Bundy • Evan Burton • Michael Byers • Christine Byl • Gerard Byrne • Jack Cady • Annie Callan • Kevin Canty • Peter Carey • Ron Carlson • Brian Champeau • Vikram Chandra • Mike Chasar • Robert Chibka • Carolyn Chute • George Makana Clark • Dennis Clemmens • Aaron Cohen • Robert Cohen • Evan S. Connell • Ellen Cooney • Rand Richards Cooper • Rita D. Costello • Wendy Counsil • William J. Cyr • Tristan Davies • Toi Derricotte • Janet Desaulniers • Tiziana di Marina • Junot Díaz • Stephen Dixon • Matthew Doherty • Michael Dorris • Siobhan Dowd • Eugenie Doyle • Tiffany Drever • Andre Dubus • Andre Dubus III • Wayne Dyer • Ron Egatz • Barbara Eiswerth • Mary Ellis • Susan Engberg • Lin Enger • James English • Tony Eprile • Louise Erdrich • Zoë Evamy • Nomi Eve • Edward Falco • Merrill Feitell • Lisa Fetchko • Susan Fox • Michael Frank • Pete Fromm • Daniel Gabriel • Ernest Gaines • Tess Gallagher • Louis Gallo • Kent Gardien • Ellen Gilchrist • Mary Gordon • Peter Gordon • Elizabeth Graver • Andrew Sean Greer • Gail Greiner • John Griesemer • Paul Griner • Patricia Hampl • Christian Hansen • Elizabeth Logan Harris • Marina Harris • Erin Hart • Daniel Hayes • David Haynes • Daniel Hecht • Ursula Hegi • Amy Hempel • Andee Hochman • Alice Hoffman • Jack Holland • Noy Holland • Lucy Honig • Ann Hood • Linda Hornbuckle • David Huddle • Siri Hustvedt • Stewart David Ikeda • Lawson Fusao Inada • Elizabeth Inness-Brown • Debra Innocenti • Bruce Jacobson • Andrea Jeyaveeran • Charles Johnson • Leslie Johnson • Wayne Johnson • Thom Jones • Tom Miller Juvik • Cyril Jones-Kellet • Elizabeth Judd • Jiri Kajanë • Hester Kaplan • Wayne Karlin • Tom Kealey • Andrea King Kelly • Thomas E. Kennedy • Tim Keppel • Jamaica Kincaid • Lily King • Maina wa Kinyatti • Carolyn Kizer • Carrie Knowles • David Koon • Karen Kovacik • Jake Kreilkamp • Marilyn Krysl • Frances Kuffel • Anatoly Kurchatkin • Victoria Lancelotta • Jennifer Levasseur • Doug Lawson • Don Lee • Peter Lefcourt • Jon Leon • Doris Lessing • Debra Levy • Janice Levy • Christine Liotta • Rosina Lippi-Green • David Long • Nathan Long • Salvatore Diego Lopez • Melissa Lowver • William Luvaas • Richard Lyons • Bruce Machart • Jeff MacNelly • R. Kevin Maler • George Manner • Jana Martin • Lee Martin • Alice Mattison • Jane McCafferty • Judith McClain • Cammie McGovern • Eileen McGuire • Susan McInnis • Gregory McNamee • Jenny Drake McPhee • Frank Michel • Nancy Middleton • Alyce Miller • Katherine Min • Mary McGarry Morris • Mary Morrissy • Bernard Mulligan • Abdelrahman Munif • Manuel Muñoz • Karen Munro • Kent Nelson • Sigrid Nunez • Ron Nyren • Joyce Carol Oates • Tim O'Brien • Vana O'Brien • Mary O'Dell • Chris Offutt • Laura Oliver • Felicia Olivera • Stewart O'Nan • Elizabeth Oness • Karen Outen • Mary Overton • Patricia Page • Ann Pancake • Peter Parsons • Roy Parvin • Karenmary Penn • Susan Perabo • Constance Pierce • Steven Polansky • John Prendergast • Jessica Printz • E. Annie Proulx • Kevin Rabalais • Jonathan Raban • George Rabasa • Margo Rabb • Mark Rader • Paul Rawlins • Nancy Reisman • Linda Reynolds • Kurt Rheinheimer • Carol Roh-Spaulding • Anne Rice • Michelle Richmond • Alberto Ríos • Roxana Robinson • Paulette Roeske • Stan Rogal • Frank Ronan • Elizabeth Rosen • Janice Rosenberg • Jane Rosenzweig • Karen Sagstetter • Kiran Kaur Saini • Mark Salzman • Carl Schaffer • Libby Schmais • Natalie Schoen • Jim Schumock • Lynn Sharon Schwartz • Barbara Scot • Amy Selwyn • Catherine Seto • Bob Shacochis • Evelyn Sharenov • Sally Shivnan • Ami Silber • Al Sim • George Singleton • Floyd Skloot • Roland Sodowsky • R. Clifton Spargo • Gregory Spatz • Brent Spencer • L.M. Spencer • Lara Stapleton • Barbara Stevens • John Stinson • George Stolz • William Styron • Karen Swenson • Liz Szabla • Paul Theroux • Abigail Thomas • Randolph Thomas • Joyce Thompson • Patrick Tierney • Andrew Toos • Patricia Traxler • Jessica Treadway • Rob Trucks • Kathryn Trueblood • Carol Turner • Christine Turner • Kathleen Tyau • Michael Upchurch • Lee Upton • Gerard Varni • A. J. Verdelle • Daniel Villasenor • Sergio Gabriel Waisman • Daniel Wallace • Ren Wanding • Mary Yukari Waters • Jamie Weisman • Lance Weller • Ed Weyhing • Joan Wickersham • Lex Williford • Gary Wilson • Robin Winick • Terry Wolverton • Monica Wood • Christopher Woods • wormser • Celia Wren • Calvin Wright • Brennen Wysong • Jane Zwinger

Edie Brown's parents, Oscar and Lena Ebe

Coming soon:

The world divides into the people you tell your secrets to and those you don't. And it further divides into the people you only tell a few secrets to and those who know them all.
from "Correspondence" by Laurence deLooze

He prayed that at the end of all the cows and cornfields of Nebraska, the empty, mountainous expanse of Wyoming would make things better. Perhaps the higher elevation would bring them all a bit closer to God.
from "The Great Salt Lake Desert" by Aaron Tillman

It is 1915, and he is serving just east of Suvla Bay, a few kilometers from Anzac Cove and the fighting. It is August, and the sea kicks the linen scent of its salt into the air each day, a scent that is mixed with something else, with the sweet reek of decay and raw blood.
from "Still Life" by Pauls Toutonghi

The fact that it takes so long to write a novel, years, other people find that kind of forbidding. But to me it means I get to work in the same world and enter this imaginary place for a long period of time. I like that.
from an interview with Valerie Martin by Janet Benton

Lucy's pink formica kitchen seems freeze-dried in the 1950s, the pink countertops and white tile floors speckled in stardust, as if it had been her own private dance hall where she warmed up friends and family leftovers.
from "The Healing Power of Garlic" by Jo-Ann Graziano